# THE
# RASMUSSEN
# PAPERS

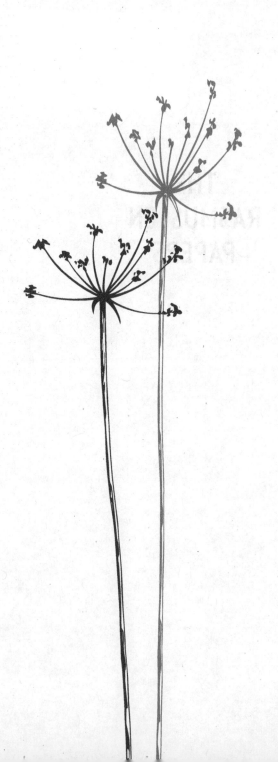

# THE RASMUSSEN PAPERS

## Connie Gault

Thistledown
Press

Thistledown Press Ltd.
Unit 222, 220 20th Street W
Saskatoon, SK S7M 0W9
www.thistledownpress.com

Library and Archives Canada Cataloguing in Publication
Title: The Rasmussen papers / Connie Gault.
Names: Gault, Connie, 1949- author.
Identifiers: Canadiana 20230569161 | ISBN 9781771872539 (softcover)
Classification: LCC PS8577.I3 D43 2021 | DDC jC813/.54—dc23

Cover and book design by Jennifer Lum
Printed and bound in Canada

Thistledown Press gratefully acknowledges the financial assistance of The
Canada Council for the Arts, SK Arts, and the government of Canada for its
publishing program.

Canada Council Conseil des arts
for the Arts du Canada

Saskatchewan

Funded by the Government of Canada    Financé par le gouvernement du Canada | Canadá

*For Joan Givner*

"If you write books don't you sell them?"

"Do you mean don't people buy them? A little—not so much
as I could wish. Writing books, unless one be a great genius—
and even then!—is the last road to fortune. I think there is no
more money to be made by literature."

Henry James
*The Aspern Papers*
1888

# { 1 }

MY FRIEND HAD done something different with her eyebrows the day we met for lunch, and it was making me pay more attention than usual to her face. I think as well as plucking them she had shaved them a bit, or maybe she'd been to a cosmetician to have them shaped. The change opened her up, gave her an attractive, puckish look. She seemed ready at any moment to smirk at something I said. It also looked as if she anticipated sharing the joke with me, although presumably neither of us yet knew what it was.

This friend has a sympathetic face and she is a good listener when she listens, but there are times when she sinks into her own world, and I was aware, by the time we received our meals, that she had drifted somewhere a little off. She had already heard a lot about my Toronto stay and the whole convoluted situation I'd encountered there. She had heard enough.

"You should read *The Aspern Papers*," she said. "Henry James."

I thought she'd stopped listening to me, but no; subtly, wryly, she was telling me her little appropriate joke. I was fond of Henry James; the next day I obtained and devoured the book. The experience of reading it was so like looking into a mirror that I decided to write my own account as a way of discovering what, sifting the weeks of my similar pursuit, I might still have to learn. I would use his plot is what I mean. I didn't forget that the image you see in a mirror is reversed. I would write a woman's version. It was fun contemplating setting out in the lively manner of the Master. I had no trouble knowing where to begin.

# { 2 }

I DIDN'T EXPECT Ryan Benson would be the one to solve my problem. I hadn't thought he'd interest himself in my venture and might not have mentioned it if we hadn't run out of conversation so soon. He was only interviewing me for a small spot in an already mostly written article on regionalism in Canadian literature. There was little to say on the topic that hadn't been said before, and he didn't pretend for a second that I would add anything important to the discussion. Although I had written a book of essays on one of Western Canada's finest poets, he stopped taking notes before we'd drained our chai lattes. That made a total of two notes in his quaint leather-bound notebook (not his only affectation; another was a lemon yellow silk scarf knotted at his neck). One note was only the date and my name, and the other was a pithy comment marked end to end with those little squiggles that meant I would—not for the first time—live to regret giving my opinion. Together, after those jottings, we stared out the window and watched the passersby on far Queen West, many of them with neon hair, bondage-grade chains, and leather bits. Oh yes, and tattoos, planted up their arms like succulents. There were also those who attracted attention more originally and less voluntarily with odd tics, grimaces, and gaucheries. They were more my kind, the ones who looked about to trip at any moment, with nothing as solid as a sidewalk to land on.

And then I asked Ryan Benson if by any chance he knew anything about old Aubrey Ash, who was rumoured to have been Marianne Rasmussen's lover.

That sparked him. "You know the story?" he asked. "How the two of them, Marianne and Aubrey, were caught dancing together late one night, at a writers' retreat—in the nude?"

Marianne and Aubrey, he called them, as if he'd known them well in their heyday. They were *caught*, he said, and I thought, like bugs in amber, although the light would have been silver.

"It was back in the sixties," he said.

"Those wild sixties," I said.

It was an old story and not remarkable as scandals go, but it happened that the two of them danced on the moonlit grounds of a Benedictine abbey, that night so long ago, and the image of their blithe bodies waltzing over the shadowy grass, under the looming bell tower, had proved irresistible and kept it in circulation all these years.

"I'd love to meet him," I said. "But no one seems to be able to tell me if he's alive or dead."

A boyish look crossed Ryan's face. He leapt to his feet, took hold of my arm, and steered me out of the café.

"What?" I said.

"I'll take you to him." He still had hold of my arm, and a good thing too; I wasn't used to sidewalk traffic like we encountered on far Queen West. In spite of my own excitement (I stopped breathing when he said he could take me to Aubrey

Ash), I was distracted enough to slow down and gawk. He was having none of that. "With the element of surprise, we might get in to see him," he said, sounding like both the Hardy boys at once.

"Where are we going?" I asked as he dragged me onto a streetcar.

"Cabbagetown," he said.

———————

Definitely it would have been too far to walk. Ryan gallantly found me a seat, a single on the left side of the ancient and alarmingly dirty car. He stayed beside me when we took off, swaying elegantly without having to hold onto strap or pole. I liked him better now that I saw he'd ridden public transit often enough to be able to perform that feat. Watching him while he gazed into his phone, I realized I was bewildered as to his age, although obviously he was younger than I. He might be anywhere between thirty and forty-five. I was anywhere between fifty and sixty-five; I mean time had not altered me in my own mind. Ryan's youthfulness ascended as we clattered and lurched eastward and enthusiasm overcame his need to prove his urban creative class credentials. I smiled up at him; it was like pressing the chest of a talking doll. His mouth opened, his bright eyes engaged mine, he seemed eager to speak, but first he glanced over each shoulder, scanning faces for any that might be familiar, I suppose, for any of our sort who might hear and appreciate the information he had to impart. He found only the working poor, most of them dressed with no nod towards fashion and some of them elderly, but even so he leaned towards me and surreptitiously murmured the few details that were too deli-cious to be kept unshared.

You would have thought he was offering the last map to the Holy Grail, with stops for pleasant improprieties marked along the way. I wish he had been, but his information was current, and the subject was old. Here is what Ryan Benson told me about Aubrey Ash, who had been a short story writer of some national influence without ever producing a book that sold over a thousand copies, and those copies only to students and other writers, a classic case of a writers' writer: that he had fallen on hard times in his old age and was liv-ing with his brother, yes actually living with his brother in his brother's townhouse in Cabbagetown, and get this—their financial situation had become so perilous, they rented out rooms on Airbnb.

"How did I not know this?" I asked, and dear Ryan (I was getting fond of him) tapped his nose, just like a character who'd marched, beaming, out of any of Charles Dickens' nov-els, precisely to lighten my life. He didn't seem to mind that I laughed at him. Maybe he was being funny on purpose. But it was sad to think that Aubrey Ash, who had once basked in Marianne Rasmussen's presence, was now living in pen-ury and obscurity, that he was now discussed—if at all—as if dead, that he was living out his last days in a dilapidated old townhouse in an out-of-the-way cul-de-sac in the semi-gen-trified, semi-slummish part of Cabbagetown. According to Ryan, some years ago a great change had come over the once gregarious Ash, and no one knew why it was that he had become reclusive unless it was that proximity had rendered him similar to his brother, a humble unemployed architect who had never been one for the limelight that the author had for decades craved.

"I feel lucky," I said, looking up at Ryan, "to have stumbled on the very person who can help me find the very writer I want to interview."

"Don't you love coincidences?" Ryan said, his voice rising to a high note with that last word. "But it's not really a coincidence, you know. I have read that book you wrote, you know. The essays. On Marianne Rasmussen. I looked you up in preparation for today."

I could not help feeling flattered. A journalist in Toronto had read my work, or at least thought highly enough of me to pretend he had.

"Thinking about Rasmussen got me interested in Ash," he said. "I hoped to interview him myself. Thought there might be an article in it, sob story angle. But it wasn't to be. Turned down at the door. I met the brother though. You'll like him, I think."

It had no doubt taken considerable detective work to find the Ash brothers; I congratulated Ryan on his resourcefulness. He was pleased to give the details. Having heard rumours of their whereabouts, but with no actual address, he'd perused the several websites devoted to the neighbourhood of Cabbagetown, both present day and historical. He looked for any literary references and found mention of the house where Frank Graham, an earlier Canadian writer, had lived for several years. Acting on a hunch, he went to the house one day and knocked on the door. "*Et voila!*" The brother who answered couldn't deny who he was; his vigorous and white-maned masculinity, even in extreme old age (he would be at least eighty, Ryan thought) proclaimed him an Ash on sight.

"Amazing," I said.

"Pure intuition. They would have known Frank Graham; the Toronto literary society was tiny in those days. I knew

7

they owned a house in Cabbagetown. Maybe they bought it from him."

"And they did."

"They did. And now their circumstances are dire, you know."

"But they own the house? They could sell it and live on the proceeds? Property values in the area must be high."

"Unsellable. It's a duplex and the other side, which of course they don't own, is literally falling down. Their half isn't much better, truth be told."

Truth be told, a superannuated phrase to come from the hip lips of such as Ryan; I'd thought the silk scarf a fashionable accessory as well as too warm for what was turning out to be a hot day, but maybe it was a throwback. And if the truth has to be told, I thought Ryan Benson didn't have a clue. He took Ash for the real thing; I knew it was Rasmussen. Aubrey Ash was important to me, however, because he might have the map to my kind of Holy Grail. There was a gap in Marianne Rasmussen's archives; I believed Aubrey Ash had letters and perhaps other papers, drafts of poems—it could be anything Marianne Rasmussen had written—that could reveal the genesis of her Flesh Poems. That belief was my whole reason for being in Toronto, for being on this streetcar.

Ryan said he had not been admitted; the brother had stood in the doorway, taking up almost all the space of the doorway so that Ryan could glimpse only a patch of dingy wallpaper and down the hall the high ceiling with ornate mouldings common to those old townhouses built in the early 1900s. I didn't see how he thought I'd fare any better than he had.

"Ah, there's a difference between us," he said. "I went to their door hoping to get an interview. You're going to do them a favour."

"I think you're being very optimistic on my behalf."

"Ah. I don't mean what you're really after, you know, the book you want to write. That would be no favour. I mean you'll come to them asking for a place to rent."

"But I'm not. I'm not looking for a place to rent. I'm going home at the end of the week."

"I told you, they've got rooms, a basement suite I think it is, listed on Airbnb."

"Anyway, I couldn't afford it."

"Look at it this way: can you afford not to? How else are you going to get to know the old guy and talk to him long enough to get material? Think about it. He must have letters, photos—could be a treasure trove. Live with them. It's the perfect answer."

"Why didn't you?"

"I am curious about them," he admitted. "But not to the extent you are."

Half a dozen kids with backpacks surged between us then, giving me a few seconds to ruminate on the things he'd said. As soon as I had him beaming in my sights again, I asked, "How do you know how curious I am?"

"Easy. It's written all over your face."

"Then I'd better erase it before we get there," I said, and I began right there, while we jolted along, practising making my face blank, because it would never do to show how much I cared. It's never smart to show you care; that's a lesson to learn and learn again. And Ryan was right. I was more than curious. Marianne Rasmussen's poetry took off after she left Aubrey Ash. I wanted to know why, how. I wanted to know everything it was humanly possible to know about the affair between the two of them, how it began, how it progressed, and even more, how it ended.

"You haven't achieved erasure," Ryan said, plainly amused at my attempts.

"What a word to use. You frighten me."

"Yes, it would be the last thing a biographer would want to hear. But you used it first," he reminded me.

I shivered.

"Someone tread on your grave?" he asked.

"A goose," I said, meaning him, and he laughed. It seemed we were friends, but I did not think I would trust him too far.

"You are planning to write Rasmussen's biography, aren't you?" he asked as the streetcar lurched again to a stop. He ushered me to the exit. "It's your logical next step," he said, indicating the steps to the ground.

———————

A new thought came to me when we descended at Queen and Ontario. Could Marianne Rasmussen have visited the Ash house? Ryan said it was located a few blocks north; I gazed as far as I could see up those few blocks and wondered. Could she have walked on this same street, on this same sidewalk I was standing on? I gazed down at my old Birkenstocks and imagined the strappy sixties sandals she would have worn on her slender, tanned feet.

Our shortened shadows walked with us when we crossed the intersection to a corner store that looked as if it belonged in a third world country. (*Convenience*, the faded sign proclaimed, and I guessed that would be its only plus.) But I wasn't paying a lot of attention to details; I was trying to see the present overlaid with the past. I was in love with the idea that Rasmussen's shadow might have slid along this same pavement decades before us. Ryan didn't think so. "Unless they had a tryst here," he said.

"What a lovely, old-fashioned word."

Ryan ignored my attempt at a little dig. "Aubrey didn't move in with Harold that long ago. I mean it was years ago, but relative to his age not that long ago. He lived in Victoria and then Halifax before returning to Toronto. But of course he might have visited Harold in that time. So it's not impossible that she might have visited him here, just unlikely."

We dropped in to the store for water but didn't buy any because as soon as we entered through the propped-open corner doorway, we were bombarded. The entire little establishment reeked of urine. It was so bad the owners apologized and pointed to the back wall, where a clerk was trying to shoo a dirty and dishevelled old woman out a side door. A hoary, ropy old thing, in grim layers of clothing, maybe all she owned and possibly, going by the state of them, stuck in degrees to her skin, she was objecting, in definitive language, to being ejected. Shovels full of matted grey hair fanned down almost to her waist and got in the way of the fellow who was trying to oust her. At one point, one of his hands got so tangled in her hair it jerked her backwards and they tumbled together into the glass doors of the refrigerator compartment and slid down to the floor.

"Whew," Ryan and I said to each other as soon as we hit fresh air. It felt like an escape, like a blessing, really, to be out in the air. Soon after us, the old woman emerged, yelling a string of curses she'd evidently refined over time. It was a creative effort, I thought, an improvement on the might-have-been-expected commentary such as where the poor man ousting her might put a part of his anatomy as far as she was concerned. At one point she called him a rump-fed runion. "Almost Shakespearean," I said to Ryan. "Poor thing." We agreed on that as we hurried away.

---

It was a seedy area, the buildings unkempt, the denizens to match. Cars zoomed past us, the drivers eager to be gone as fast as their wheels would take them, yet even here, where the few people who passed us on the sidewalks staggered, and where one humble fellow lay flat out on a patchy lawn with a bottle beside him and the hot sun beating down on his face—his mouth gaping as if it would exhale his life all at once if it could—the odd refurbished house gleamed among the neglected, and as we progressed farther north the character of the street changed drastically. Almost every house had been tarted up to meet the standards of the BMWs and Porsches and Lexus SUVs parked on the street under the branches of sheltering trees. The same couldn't be said, however, for the tall townhouse we stopped before. The entire half that Ryan pointed out as belonging to the Ash brothers slumped in a portrait of despair, and with good reason: its twin clung to it and dragged it down.

"It's not really Cabbagetown. Well, it's on the edge of Cabbagetown," Ryan said.

I gathered that being on the edge was something like being from Saskatchewan. Easy to see we weren't in the tony district of the city, however much some residents were trying. Weeds flourished among the overgrown shrubs in the small, shared front garden, the twin paths hadn't been swept in months or years, and garbage in the you-name-it form of disposable coffee cups, plastic bags, candy wrappers, condoms, cigarette butts, hypodermic syringes, and other remains of a few drug kits (we stood there for a while) nestled in the nooks and crannies of the vegetation. The wooden steps leading to the Ash brothers' door looked to be rotting; none led to the twin's door where boards had been slapped across a broken window. Obviously, half the building was uninhabited and uninhabitable. The No Trespassing, No Loitering sign posted on the door could go unread; the place was condemned for good reason. Yet in spite of all that, it seemed to me, fancifully, that in the play of light and shadow across the old bricks, in the breeze that lifted the overgrown ferns and made them wave as if they had something to say if only they could say it, the spirit of Marianne Rasmussen hovered. I mentioned to Ryan my feeling that she must have been here; at least once she must have come to this house. Or why would I feel her presence so strongly? In the sighing of the tree branches over our heads I could almost hear her intimate, confiding, cajoling voice.

"People do tend to leave their essence behind them," Ryan replied with a stress on "essence" and a mischievous sparkle in his eyes. I was annoyed. I didn't want to buck my idolatry and now because of him I was smelling the tang of urine, enclosed and intense, all over again. At least it meant I didn't have to wipe my eagerness off my face; it was disgust I had to erase as we walked up to the door. But then I noticed I was alone. I had set one foot gingerly on the bottom step and turned quickly in time to see Ryan Benson hotfooting it northward towards College Street. Ridiculously, I felt abandoned, and with my foot still up on the insecure bottom step of the Ash brothers' house, I hesitated, watching him get smaller. Maybe, I thought, I should wait a few days and marshal my strength before tackling such an enormous undertaking. And the twin house, to my left, a shambles if there ever was one, had to be a factor in my thinking; the Ash brothers weren't twins, but the analogy might hold. My research said there were nineteen years between them; if Harold was eighty, then Aubrey must be almost a hundred. It's a scary thing to contemplate meeting a person that old, to say nothing of attempting to persuade him to tell you his secrets and let you read love letters he'd received from a brilliant and outspoken poet. It was the last thought that swayed me. My quest had its own nobility. I was only to be a messenger, bringing Marianne Rasmussen to the world. I heard her whisper to me when I reminded myself of that; it wasn't just the leaves fussing above me. She sounded like a confident big sister giving me advice I couldn't quite hear.

I had already done as much with my research as I could. I'd written about her in periodicals and anthologies. I'd based my first book of essays on her poems. I'd done all that to boost her reputation. Now I could do more. So I stepped up to that door.

My knock might have been timid; I waited some time for an answer, not wishing to appear impatient and thinking again of the age of the residents. I didn't want to make either of the men hurry. These old three-storey townhouses would have steep stairs; how awful it would be to cause a terrible fall. While I stood there, I diverted myself from imagining that bone-cracking plummet from the top of a flight to the bottom by thinking over the time I'd spent with Ryan Benson. In spite of his efforts to put me in my place, I had enjoyed his company from the start. I hadn't taken his condescension personally. But because I'd observed it, and because he was young (or youngish) and male, I'd hardly expected him to regard Marianne Rasmussen with the same reverence I felt for her. I'd been sure he would imply, or come right out and state, as men had before him, that she was a woman's poet, as if there could be such a thing as a gendered poet, a limited poet, when a mind as capacious and searching—and witty— as hers was considered. But no, walking to the brothers' house, he'd concurred with me; she was pre-eminent in his mind too. The awe in his voice when he said her name spoke as decisively as his words; she was firmly ensconced in his canon. With energy, remembering this, I banged on the door.

As I stood sucking my knuckles on that precarious stoop, my hurting hand reminded me that Rasmussen was said to have hurt Ash, and badly. She had left him abruptly, without any warning. He wasn't the only guy she'd dumped without compunction, but as far as I knew he was the only one still alive. My heart rate increased, thinking of meeting him, as much as it would have years before, when I was a kid, no matter how hopelessly I would have viewed any possible liaison with such a sexually provocative older man. Never as beautiful, even in rosy youth, or as talented, or as bold as Marianne Rasmussen, I would not have had a chance with Aubrey Ash. But we might meet as equals now, Aubrey and I, sharing our adulation of the poet and our mutual pain at loving her, because it was painful for me too, to adore some- one so far above me. In a strange way, her behaviour towards both of us had been undeniably shabby, even one might say brutal. The difference was that in his case her actions had been deliberate; in my case, since she had never known of my existence, her cruel supremacy was entirely involuntary.

The big question was whether or not he would have for- given her. I had. She could not help being a bright star above us all. For his part, he might consider that many men had desired her, hunted her, literally sometimes stalked her, that

15

she'd had her pick of lovers, and that it would have been hard to resist the admiration and the magnetism of sexual intrigue, not to mention the yearning for real love that sent an electric charge through some of her lines. As for her dropping lovers when they no longer interested her, it seemed to me that men weren't known for taking care in letting women down.

I banged again on the door, this time with the side of my fist, and as I did so there rose before me, laid on top of the old panelled wood, the impressive head of Aubrey Ash, in grainy grey and silver, as it was portrayed in the black-and-white photograph in the back of his later books, complete with wild hair, insinuating eyes, and sensual lips, and trimmed at the neck with an eighties-era gold chain. The thought that I could soon look into those eyes that had once looked into the eyes of Marianne Rasmussen, eyes that had seen an answer there, a response, the flicker of effulgent recognition, that thought fired me up, and I banged again, and so when the door opened I had my fist raised.

# { 3 }

THE DOOR OPENED and Harold Ash appeared and smiled on me. He smiled on me as if cymbals had crashed to announce my arrival and he wondered what all the excitement was about until he saw me and then he knew. That glorious welcoming smile. I had to say something, I had to articulate some reason for knocking several times peremptorily on his door, so I said what Ryan Benson had suggested I say: "I believe you have a room or a suite for rent?" I don't know if I would have had the courage to ask if it hadn't been for his smile, and even as I spoke I recalled I had not seen basement windows at the front of the house. For a full minute (or it seemed that long), Harry Ash gazed at me, waiting. "Airbnb?" I added in a smaller voice. "You advertised?"

"Come in," he said, and a thrill shivered through me.

I've forgotten to say that he seemed to me to be a beautiful specimen of a man, very like his older brother, or I should say like the photos of his older brother: the white shock of hair, the intense blue-eyed stare, and the lovely lips, but without the gold chain. His beard was neatly trimmed; he wore a loose black T-shirt, blue jeans, and sandals (Birkenstocks, I noticed). In spite of his age he carried himself, I thought, like a tall pine overlooking a lonely lake. He was a man I would follow anywhere, instinctively, although with the unflattering suspicion that wherever we went together I would be trotting at his heels.

The house: the wallpaper was dingy, as Ryan had said; it was that no-colour colour, sort-of brown, that might have been original. The ceilings were high and the mouldings as ornate as working-class plasterers could make them and middle-class buyers could afford. Once this dwelling would have housed a man and his wife and eight or nine kids, and cabbages would have grown in place of shrubs and ferns, if legend could be believed. (I think I am wrong about that; the famed vegetable gardens likely grew in the front yards of more humble dwellings, the tiny workmen's cottages to be found on other blocks farther into the neighbourhood, where any cabbages planted nowadays were ornamental.) No lights were on in the elegant old fixtures in the hall, or in the dim rooms we passed to the left of the hallway, or in the vertiginous stairwell to the right. Harry led me into the kitchen, where a square of half-hearted sunlight tried to illuminate a table and chairs set against the far wall. The air was close, all the windows being shut against the heat of the day, and there was, as I'd expected given Ryan's description of the brothers' poverty, no hint of the air conditioning ubiquitous in Toronto homes.

Harry indicated that I should take a seat at the table. With the feeling that this was all happening too easily, and with trepidation in case I wasn't able to play my role adequately now that I was inside the house, I sat myself down at that table. Immediately, surreptitiously (or so I believed), I sought the back door through which I could exit if I needed to escape. An honest-sounding explanation, now that more than my foot was in the door, was urgently required. Luckily,

18

just then I noticed that Harry Ash's look of outstanding good health (given his age) was aided by what appeared to be the glow of a slight sunburn, and I turned to the window. "You have a backyard," I blurted. "How lovely. How perfect." It was like drinking a glass of cold water, I was so refreshed by the sight of the tangled greenery and by the intuition of what that little patch of earth could do for me. "It's simply perfect. You will let me use it, won't you?" I could sunbathe there, I thought, and felt myself blushing. There was nothing I liked better than sunbathing in the nude, but it was hardly the sort of thing to reveal on meeting a prospective landlord. As quickly as I could, I went on. "A quiet outdoor space, a real garden, is exactly what I need. I have a lot of work to finish this summer, and I could take my laptop out there, couldn't I? Please say yes. It would be so good for me."

The garden I could see from the window was no Eden, but it must have been a pleasant retreat years before it grew into a convoluted mass of bushes and vines and whatever else had a mind to flourish there. "There's space for a chair and a small table, or I could carve some space," I pointed out. And there was that smile again. Here I must confess that although I was bowled over by Harry at first sight, I'd also planned, while waiting for him to answer the door, that he would become infatuated with me, and that this infatuation would lead him to be able to deny me nothing. How did I believe I could accomplish this coup? There was the age difference, to begin with—that alone should be enough to give me an advantage—and there was his supposed isolation too, easy to include as a factor, propinquity being a known ingredient in affairs of the heart. And ever since high school I'd real-ized that boys and men found me cute. They responded well to my cheeky disregard of their culturally assigned superior status. The good-looking, nonchalant types especially found me disarmingly agreeable; in fact, I was so often successful with them I had to remind myself sometimes not to get coy.

"I'm sorry," I said. "Am I getting ahead of myself? Just the idea of sitting in that green space, with the birds the only distraction, the thought of working there in the luxurious summer air has me feeling so happy, I—but I suppose you and your family use it? I could set a time, a limited time to sit there, if you like. Or of course, you could. Set the limits, I mean. You and your family could let me know what times of day would be appropriate."

He sat far back in his chair as if to see me more clearly. I didn't blink even though he gazed at me for several seconds without speaking, and then he slowly shook his head. "You might be getting ahead of yourself," he said. Oh, he was lovely to look at, leaning back like that in that assessing pose. After that charged pause—and obviously he was going to wait for me to speak, however long it took—I said, "I could do a little gardening for you, if you like. The front as well as the back. I have a bit of a green thumb."

He laughed at that. "Do you?" he said.

He'd laughed at me; that meant the ground was getting firmer under my feet. And he had freckles, I noted, and they always seemed signs of friendliness to me. "Mostly for arranging things, cleaning up, clearing up, and rearranging. I have a good eye," I said. "For placement of plantings. And all that. Or so I've been told."

"You haven't told me your name," he said.

I wondered at that, what the link in his mind had been between my avowal of organizational prowess and his wanting to know my name. Did he guess I was a writer, editor, and biographer, one of those tidiers of words and hearts and minds and motivations? If he did, he would likely kick me out just when I had insinuated myself into his kitchen, so I gave him a false name, and fearing that I might forget one entirely unrelated to me, I gave him my mother's. It had been a few months since she'd died but she was still often on my mind. Just saying her name out loud made me crave a drink; she was rarely without a whiskey and water, certainly not after three in the afternoon. "I don't know your name either," I ventured.

"Wasn't it in the advertisement? The one for the Airbnb room or suite we have available for rent?" he asked with a glint that brightened his blue eyes.

He had made the question seem a little humorous and not completely mocking, but I didn't because of that think it wasn't barbed. In this instance the truth seemed a wise choice. "I didn't actually see your ad. I was told about it."

"And given the address? So you came here on the chance it might be suitable?" He spoke seriously, as if he wanted to know my answer, but I felt his impulse might have been sarcastic; I would have had to agree, if we could have spoken our minds, that sarcasm was warranted. "The neighbourhood, the grounds, the gardens, the state of the house all suit you, do they?" he went on. "They're what you're looking for?"

Since I couldn't speak my mind, I forged ahead with kudos for the neighbourhood. "And as for the house and grounds, well, to tell you the truth, I have a very small income. I'm working on a research grant at present, actually, which is why I'm here in the city at all. I do love this neighbourhood and I couldn't afford the rent for one of the... " I'd been about to say one of the better houses and didn't know how to proceed without causing offence. He didn't help me out and I turned again to the garden. "The thought of working in a garden, you know..." Then, like another glass of water tilted to my lips (on such a hot day, you would have thought he'd have offered a drink), I remembered the perfect thing Ryan Benson had told me. "And what drew me, initially, was that I did some research into the area, and discovered this was once Frank Graham's house." I halted as if in reverence, and got no response. "I'm a reader and a fan of CanLit. It's unfashionable to say that these days, but I am, and the chance to live in his house, well, it intrigued me."

"You're a writer," he said.

"Oh," I said.

"There are no other fans of CanLit."

"No, you're wrong. There are others."

"Not so you'd notice."

I had an opportune thought. "Are you a writer too? You must be, to say that with such—"

"I'm a nothing," he said. "My brother was a writer."

"Was?"

"He's too old now. For writing or anything else. He'll be a hundred next month, if he lasts that long. He lives upstairs, never comes down. Does not require any minutes or hours in the garden. If we decide to let you stay, you could help me look after him."

How he smiled at the look of horror that must have stayed stamped on my face for a full minute. Gardening I could offer, even housework of a limited style, and cooking—I like to cook—but looking after an old man? I nearly ran.

"We didn't advertise a room or a suite for rent. Not on Airbnb or anywhere else," he said quite sternly.

"You didn't?"

"No."

"But I was told you had. I mean, I didn't just make it up."

"Who told you? Was it Ryan Benson?"

"You know him?"

"We might call him Our Mutual Friend. Except he's no friend of mine, and if he's yours, you could find better."

"He's not a friend, only a slight acquaintance." I had forgotten Ryan said he'd met Harold Ash at the door. "But yes, he was the one who told me. So it isn't true? I mean, you have a lot of space here, a lot of rooms. Couldn't I have one or two? I'm very quiet."

I wish I could say my powers of persuasion moved Harry that day, and got him to stop wondering about my motives, but I could see it was for some reason of his own that he decided to let his inquiry drop. I guess I didn't look much of a threat. He said, "I'll confer with my brother."

"Now?"

"Now? Patience isn't one of your virtues."

It wasn't, and neither was the concept of quitting when you're ahead. "I feel a bit silly asking this again," I said, "but I don't in fact know your names." It was a mistake, and one that should have served as a warning. As soon as I said I didn't know their names, for the heaven's-sake second time, I remembered that Ryan had requested an interview with Aubrey Ash. As night follows day, and especially with me being the big fan of CanLit, he would have told me the brothers' names. My face burned with the shame Harry's gaze bestowed on me. But he said nothing, not a word; he didn't remonstrate and he didn't deign to tell me their names. He stood up, set his chair back neatly into the table, and left the kitchen. I listened to his tread while he climbed the two flights up to the third floor, and gradually I came to understand a fact that would become clearer later on: that although the brothers lived like hermits, apart from society, they knew they were known; they knew it and they liked it and they were not at all averse to having it affirmed. It was a moving realization for me. After all, I was only in this house because of my desire to cement Marianne Rasmussen's fame. It seemed then that I'd missed an opportunity, I should have said right out who I was, or perhaps not right out; the whole truth wouldn't do. There was no reason Aubrey Ash would want to contribute to a biography of Marianne Rasmussen and add to her reputation. If I'd been smart (and unethical, but the two sometimes go together), I would have declared myself *his* wannabe biographer. I could have done it abashedly, as if the truth had to be squirmed out of me, so Harry would have been charmed; he would have wanted of his own accord to bound up all those stairs and urge his old brother to welcome me with open arms.

While I waited for Harry's return, and once I'd run out of should-have-dones, I looked around the kitchen, which was of a good size and well supplied with cupboards and counters. The fridge and stove were old but seemed to be in working condition, and all was as clean as a good cook would wish. I was a good cook. It was another inducement I could offer: maybe I could supply the meals, buy groceries in lieu of rent, and wine too for dinner. It should only take a week, I figured, my spirits rising, to wrap old Harry's heart in tissue paper and tie it with a bow, and with his help to persuade old Aubrey to part with whatever documents he had. With that prospect in mind, I got up and wandered into the hall and then into the two joined rooms off the hall, a dining room and living room. An antique table and chairs of solid quality, heavily coated with dust, reigned in the dining room under an enormous chandelier. The living room furniture was worn, and although the room appeared unused I felt I could distinguish the outlines, the absences, of bodies that had sat there exchanging deep and meaningful conversation.

Both of the reception rooms had fireplaces on the far walls that so fired my imagination I soon lit logs in the dining room and set the chandelier twinkling, imagining the wonderful play of light across Harry's face as he miraculously appeared at the head of the table, blessing the day I entered his house (while also pleased that his brother never came downstairs, so was left out of our intimate *tête-à-tête*). Oh, he would take Aubrey a tray, of course, lovingly prepared by me. Or I would. I really had to keep my eye on the prize. I would be the one to mount the stairs with the tray, set it down for Aubrey, make sure all was to his liking, and each time, as he contemplated eating my delicious meal, which would cater naturally to his extreme age but in the most delicate way, he would tell me a little more about himself. And once he was properly smitten, food and my dedicated kindness having done their work and taken his defences down, he would divulge all his memories of Marianne Rasmussen and show me, give me—to help me understand exactly how it had been between them, how it had started, how it had progressed, and how it had ended—her papers.

I heard Harry descending from the third floor to the second, but I didn't skitter back to the kitchen; the picture I'd painted in the dining room held me too much in thrall. I waited for him there, half in daydream.

"You'll have to come back tomorrow," he said. He stood behind me, speaking to my back. "Aubrey needs time to think about it."

I looked up to the chandelier and said, "I'm not normally a sensitive person, not given to experiencing extrasensory or paranormal stuff." This was a preamble, meant to lead into the way I really did feel, which was that I belonged in this house, but a single long ray of light just then, when I was about to say "but," made it through the film on the etched glass of the front room window and lit me where I stood. I could hardly believe it. A weird sense of awe held me completely inert for a few seconds, while the sunlight warmed me (it almost seemed as if Harry's arms were around me, as if he'd come up behind me and embraced me), and then I turned to look at him, and saw sympathy in his face. "Oh," I said. We smiled at each other like two lost beings who had just met by accident after believing themselves forever alone.

---

Ryan, when he met me the next morning in a Parliament Street coffee shop with a name something like Jolt, said, "Aubrey will say no; he won't want the chaos another person in the house would cause. Remember how old he is."

This was a turnaround for Ryan, who had after all initiated my desire to live in the Ash brothers' house, but I felt optimistic and only said, "I don't think it's going to be a problem." I ducked my head and picked at my blueberry scone.

"What? You think you made such an impression on old Harold that he'll stump for you?"

Harry, I corrected silently.

"You do think so, don't you? You think he's fallen for you and he's dying for you to return and live with him in cozy squalor."

To placate him, because he looked and sounded jealous, I chuckled right along with him. It was another hot day, and in the ecologically conscientious coffee shop no air conditioning was helping us cope. I could feel sweat rolling down my scalp under my hair, and I could see Ryan's perspiration making runnels down his neck into his already very damp and very limp silk scarf. I could tell it was hard for Ryan to contemplate my possible triumph. He was constantly tugging at his scarf (this one a subdued dotted taupe) as if it had begun to choke him. But I wasn't all that sympathetic when I remembered he'd lied to me about the brothers posting an advertisement on Airbnb. I didn't mention it, nor was I inclined to forget it. For the time being it could function as a guard to any tendency I might have to consider him a comrade.

"You'll let me know if you make inroads, if you're allowed to stay," he said at last.

"Mmm," I said, and paid for our coffees and pastries.

---

Walking is always conducive to thinking, and as I strolled the few blocks towards the brothers' house, I savoured my small victory over Ryan. The night before, assailed by doubts about what in the world I was getting into—and why in the world I would let myself get into it—I'd given myself a pep talk and decided I would forge ahead the way someone as self-confident as Marianne Rasmussen would have done. I was pleased with myself while I walked to the Ash house. I'd already made inroads with Harry. At the coffee shop I'd seen Ryan's envy. Nice girls finish last, I reminded myself when I felt guilty for my little gloat. The past couple of years had taught me a few things about toughening up and keeping cool and putting my needs first. And I could do it. I could be tough and cool; I could put my needs first because my cause was noble. Yes, for some reason that word noble was on my mind, a justification before any was really required.

By the time I reached the house on Ontario Street at the agreed upon hour of one o'clock, having waded through heat and humidity, some of my optimism had seeped away and been replaced by a fuzzy feeling I can't name; the nearest I can come to describing it would be to say I experienced a sense of suspended grief. But that seems to imply fore-knowledge of the *whoo-ee* kind that I disdain. Let's just say I approached the door and knocked in a more subdued man-ner than I had anticipated. I had to knock only once and Harry appeared as if he'd been waiting there. He seemed the same as the day before, courteous and quiet, although without the welcoming smile. As he stepped back to let me in, I felt an awkwardness arise between us that was almost physical. It seemed he made an effort to keep some distance from me. But he was reputed to be shy, I reminded myself, and it was all too possible I looked overeager.

"Come upstairs," he said and immediately started up the steep staircase to our right. I followed close behind. Light shone ahead as we ascended, it glittered in Harry's white hair, and I was reminded of the chandelier and thought it a reassuring sign. My pulse started throbbing when we turned and mounted to the third floor, and not just because all those stairs were a workout. I can feel it now, the blood coursing, the combined feelings of excitement and anxiety as I recalled that Aubrey Ash and Marianne Rasmussen were VIPs. They had written the first real wave of Canadian literature when to publish was a culturally significant undertaking.

I emerged from the stairs into a room that took up the entire third floor. There at the top of the house the ceil-ing soared, arched in a beautiful symmetry, and sunlight poured in from two skylights. It was like visiting someone in a church. And Aubrey Ash, sitting across the room, half turned away from me, showing no interest in my arrival in his sanctum, could have been a bishop. He wouldn't have looked entirely ridiculous in a pointed hat. I approached haltingly, taking in the furnishings, a bathroom that obviously had been installed some years previously, given the age of the fixtures, a kitchenette of the same vintage, a king-sized bed and bedside table, a grand fireplace. Across the room two easy chairs had a low, round table between them, piled with books and magazines. Bookshelves lined the walls to chest height, and into one a small television set had been installed. In spite of the utilitarian furniture, the room at the top of the house was a gorgeous space; it had been perfectly designed and executed to lift the spirits. The abstract paintings on the walls were not to my taste, but if a room could make you sing, this one would do it. Money is required to achieve such perfection, so money had to have come into the household some years ago, but I saw no evidence to suggest it had flowed in the past two decades. And then I was face to face with Aubrey Ash, the muse for Marianne Rasmussen's most exciting poetry.

During my walk from the coffee shop to their house that day, as hot as it was, and humid, an extra element had been at play: an incessant and capricious wind that unsettled everything in its path. First it took one direction and then another, and then it seemed to take eighteen at once. The treetops shifted constantly, every twig and leaf and blade of grass quivered, and people and their pets (dogs seemed to be as numerous as motorized chairs and scooters on Cabbagetown sidewalks) went about their business as if one misstep could make them explode. Before I'd knocked on the brothers' door, I had looked up and watched the massy top branches of two elms, survivors of the Dutch elm disease that had wiped out most of their kind, whip around as if to toss something off, some burden I couldn't see but they could feel. In my first moments in Aubrey Ash's presence, I trembled like those branches, and strangely, I believed he did too. It was because we felt Marianne. Just as it had seemed she'd been with me outside the house the first time I set eyes on it, she made herself felt in the room as soon as I stepped up to Aubrey. He knew it too. Both of us, held in abeyance, waited until the strength of the feeling she engendered ebbed, or we got used to it.

And then I realized that Harry had silently left us. Rattled at finding myself there on my own, an invader in that room, I wasn't sure I could go on with my plans. But as soon as I worried about that, the foremost hope I'd had on arriving there, the one I'd seized on when I'd contemplated this moment, this day in this house, came to me, and it came with the understanding that I'd been foiled! I couldn't look into Ash's eyes and see what Rasmussen had seen. I couldn't look into those eyes that had beheld her. I couldn't imagine her reflected in those eyes. The man was wearing sunglasses. Were they an affectation? Or did his old eyes water at any assault of light? The room bounced with light; in that room light was its own kind of joy. Sunglasses. To dim the room? Whatever the reason he wore them, the effect was that I couldn't see his eyes, no magical transference from them to me with Marianne included was going to happen, and furthermore it was going to be hard to guess his thoughts. But my inability to guess his thoughts isn't exactly why his first words—and he spoke first—astonished me.

# { 4 }

"I KNOW YOU."

He said it with some surprise and with a wide smile that took me in, as his brother's had when he'd invited me into the house. Aubrey Ash had spoken first because I was too full of pent-up emotion to speak, and after he said that, I couldn't find a thing to say. I just stared at him, at what was left of him, his sparse white fuzz, his shiny, scaly, scabby scalp, his dandruff-sprinkled Ray-Bans, the blue vein like a snake at his temple, the thousand and one wrinkles and age spots on his still weirdly attractive face, and that big smile. He was not wearing, I feel I should mention, his signature gold chain; he was attired, in spite of the heat trapped on the third floor, in a long-sleeved sweatshirt and sweatpants in a denim-like shade of blue that suited him. I supposed the chain, if he'd worn it, would have caught and tugged at his wispy beard, or perhaps by this time in his life he'd abandoned mere ornament.

"I don't remember where," he said with an appealing slowness, akin to thoughtfulness. "It was summer, wasn't it. Could it have been Saskatchewan?"

Now I was really unnerved. I couldn't see past the dark lenses of his glasses; he didn't seem to be trying to kid me, but I was certain we'd never met. Aubrey Ash was not a man you would forget.

His voice wasn't as feeble as I'd imagined it would be; it had the force of his personality behind it as well as his long history of drawing people to him and making them feel honoured to be attracted. Watching me as if from a far shore, where he existed as a beacon, he went on in the same charming, languid way. "I taught at the summer school there a few years. School for the Arts, out in the valley, the one named after the Pauline Johnson poem. Used to be a TB sanatorium. It's a long time ago."

It never happened. I was never there. And the river and valley he was talking about were named before Pauline Johnson's poem. But I said nothing; I was still too dazed to speak.

"I remember you, you were a student, it was a short story course, full of girls as they always were." From the fond expression on his face I pictured a bevy of comely lasses sitting on the floor at his feet. He was smiling to himself now, a retrospective smile; it would have been hard to give up that life. I wondered why he'd thought it necessary to retire. I was certain he could have acolytes even now if he wanted them.

His insistence, though quiet and genial, raised a quandary for me, and I considered agreeing that I had been there at the arts camp, one of his bevy. But I remembered my fiasco of the day before, when I'd bungled things by twice asking Harry their names. I wasn't good enough at lying to get away with it. On the other hand, I didn't want to flat out deny the possibility either, since it seemed my junior status, student to his teacher, was making him feel warmly towards me and could mean he would let me stay. I sat down on the chair opposite him and leaned towards him, and that was easy, that came naturally. He was a magnet of a man, and

32

his energy reached me and drew me in as if it were inevitable that I should wish to get closer to him.

The first thing I said to him was, "You remind me of a tall tree." It had been Harry who had made me visualize a Tom Thomson painting of a pine tree by a cold lake, but the brothers, in spite of the age difference, were alike. I wasn't being totally shameless in gushing; I thought it would gladden an old man's day to hear such an admission of almost involuntary admiration. Ash was, however, dismissive. Not at all pleased. His head reared back in obvious dissatisfaction. It had been the wrong thing to say—possibly because I had never seen him standing. I started babbling about the garden and how my love of their back garden had been on my mind and had made me think of a tree. I wasn't wholly convincing, but ineptitude can sometimes work in a person's favour, it can sometimes promote sympathy for the poor flounderer. His judgemental silence meant I had to keep talking, although while I went on I became hyperconscious of all the space around us and all the incredible light. We were afloat in the space, Aubrey Ash and I, and I wasn't sure which folly I was committing, that of trying to fill emptiness with blather or of clinging too tightly to my life raft's one fellow survivor. There was something about the man, with his aura of distant beatitude and undeniable hauteur, that created drama and unease. I tried to convey that I sensed none of this, that I was too innocent to pick up the hints that we were operating on two levels and I had no foothold on either. "I love working outside," I said, glancing at the walls around me without really seeing them. Vaguely, I noticed the paintings that looked like paintings I'd seen before, but as often happened to me, I was living mostly in my projections and that meant in his garden as it could be, deconstructed by me. "The movement of the air liberates my thoughts when I'm outside," I prattled. "The smells and sounds and all the green inspire me. I can work so much more happily in a garden than anywhere else, and yours is so secluded and quiet and lovely, I feel I could do anything working there."

He appeared to be extremely bored while I talked, gazing about and all but sighing, and he was obviously relieved when I abruptly ended. "Are you still writing short stories?" he asked.

"Oh," I said. "No."

"Harry said you're a writer."

"Oh, well, not fiction though."

He looked at me the way Harry had, as if gauging my moral worth. I reminded myself that I had published a book of essays. It had been well-reviewed. Criticism and biography didn't rank as high with me as fiction (or poetry, of course), but it wasn't nothing. I said, "It would be an honour for me to be here, in the house where... " I'd been about to flatter again, I'd almost said where so many great short stories had been written. But he had likely given up writing by the time he moved in here, and I would have offended him.

"Ah, right," he said. "Where Frank Graham once lived. Harry told me you knew about that. A second-rate writer, you know."

"But it's also where you live," I couldn't keep myself from saying.

"If you call this living." Half apologetically, half humanly, he shrugged.

"He won an award, didn't he? Frank Graham? For humour?"

"Hah, there's an oxymoron for you—Canadian humour. Isn't that what we're supposed to say?"

He laughed at his own joke so I did too. "I could provide references if you need them," I said, thinking it best to move the subject of residing with them front and centre. "And I'm a good lodger. Quiet, respectable, pretty easy to get along with."

"You won't like Harry's cooking."

"He'll like mine! And you will too, I promise."

"There are better gardens than ours, by far," he said.

"It's perfect for me."

"I haven't been down there for years." He sighed. He looked up and out the small, high window in the wall above the round table between us. It was as if the sky itself, the square of it that could be seen, greyed no doubt by his sunglasses, weighed on him. I hadn't lied, he was like a tree; both the brothers were, if they only knew it. They had an inner core, rooted way down in the ground of things, and a way of stretching beyond themselves too, of branching further than you could at first realize. He sighed at me the same way he'd sighed at the bit of sky, as if he recognized all too well who I was. I noticed that but gave it no thought. I was focused on what I wanted from the visit.

He said, "Harry will come soon. I asked him to leave us alone for a few minutes."

I hoped he would go on to give me his answer, whether I could stay or had to go, and I suppose I sat well forward in my chair, unconsciously, because I really was desperate to stay. Now that I knew what he could do for me, how could I write the book I needed to write without his help? And to feel so close—it would be awful to fail now. So I leaned towards him and let him see how much I needed his answer.

"I don't know if you were a good writer. I don't recall," he said.

Oh God, I thought, after all these years, after articles— and a book—published and well-received. But of course he was still seeing me as one of his students, thinking all tenterhooks I was waiting for his pronouncement on my talent.

"Maybe you should have given up long ago. But it doesn't make much difference either way." He threw that out as if words were never truer, and then, shaking his great head, he said, "You can stay. Move in today if you want. Write your little masterpiece in my garden."

I was left speechless—the bitterness and the underlying misery behind those words (oh your little masterpiece). Tears sprang up in my eyes.

"No need to get sentimental," he said. "You'll pay your way, and we need the cash, simple as that."

I nodded, still unable to trust my voice, and right then I decided I would pay my way in more ways than he could imagine; I would gain his confidence and repay it tenfold, I would write the greatest biography ever written, not just of Marianne Rasmussen but of anyone in human history, and he would have a starring role in the book. He would praise the day he let me in.

"A month's rent in advance," he said, and he named a hefty amount, considerably more than I had expected, way more than I had expected. It staggered me to think of paying so much. Although I had received a small grant to work on the project, I was barely solvent, and I hadn't expected to stay a month. Clearly he was taking advantage of me, but even so, even as I realized that, I knew I had come so far my own momentum would keep me going. Anyway, I could see now it might take that long to get what I wanted. So I agreed.

Harry walked in then and Aubrey said, "She's bringing a month's rent, in cash, tomorrow. She'll be here at noon, in time to make our lunch." He turned to me. "Better pick up groceries on your way. The cupboards are bare."

Harry didn't comment on Aubrey's remarks, and I sensed a constraint, or something sharper than constraint between them. Possibly it was only the old rivalry of brothers, I thought. The contrast between the elder and the younger was marked, more marked than it would have been if they hadn't been so similar, and no doubt the disparity would have its effect on the older. How could you not be saddened by daily seeing someone who looked like you did twenty years ago?

"No anchovies, no capers, none of that sixty-ingredients-in-every-dish crap," Aubrey called as we started down the stairs.

I looked back at Harry and he murmured, "He watches the cooking shows."

"Is it because I'm a writer?" I asked once we were on the main floor. "Is that why he decided I could stay?"

"No. I told him you'd pay more than the rent was worth."

"I'm not rich."

"I guess you're needy," Harry said, and the way he said it, with his voice almost caressing, or at the least caring, made me believe he was already fond of me.

"Needy in a manner of speaking," he went on. "As your pal Ryan Benson is too. The suite for rent was his idea. He proposed it. For himself."

"He's not my pal. And why didn't you let him stay? Why me and not him?"

He hesitated, unsure, I guessed, how to answer, and then, with a change of tone I didn't understand, he said, "Aubrey thought you'd be a better cook." He smiled down at the floor. It was an apologetic sort of smile. "He's of a generation that expects it of a woman."

"Does he really watch cooking shows?" I asked.

"He's almost given up reading. His eyes can't take the strain. So, daytime TV. Say, let's treat this as a game. What do you say?"

What I said was, "Okay." I was a bit taken aback though, because he might as well have said "I say," like an English chap, like Cary Grant stepping out of a 1940s screen to scrape and bow. But he was such an attractive man, and I expected he'd already noticed I found him so and was embarrassed by it. He would be unused to flirting, being such a recluse, that was all. I smiled to reassure him I meant him no harm and wouldn't, given his age, ask too much of him. You see, I thought I knew him, yet thinking that—a woman has to be wary—started me worrying, because actually I didn't know him at all.

It occurred to me then, as Harry was ushering me to the door, that in my eager acceptance of everything going, I had just agreed to rent a place to live, unseen. And in the basement. I didn't want to spend one second imagining how awful it might be to live down there, or even to descend those stairs. Darkness, dankness, and the vision of chains (and not gold ones; I had watched way too many Scandinavian murder series in the past few years) flooded my mind. "Oh, it's not in the basement, is it?" I said. "The suite or the room or whatever it is? I wasn't thinking, and I haven't seen... what I've rented. Maybe you have a spare room on the second floor?"

"We wouldn't put you in the basement," Harry said, and again his voice slid over my skin, and I had to steel myself to keep from shuddering the way any animal does when it finds itself poised between danger and delight. "You can have the main floor," he said. "Convenient to the kitchen."

He beckoned me to follow him down the hall, and stopping just before the kitchen, opened a door on the left, revealing a room that would have made a large bathroom if it hadn't held, besides the usual fixtures, a washer and dryer. The appliances, like the fixtures, appeared to be of the same vintage as those on the top floor, so again I calculated that about twenty years ago, Harry had some money. He must have read my mind. Leaning against the door jamb, both hands gripping the lintel, he smiled and said, "Architecture wasn't a good fit. You need to be an entrepreneur. I had the one talent, not the other. I made enough to live on, but on spec, on contract, not much of a pension out of that, not enough to fund the long retirement of two old men. Aubrey will die soon. But my money's already gone."

He'd been casual about it, but the idea that Aubrey could die any day and my project come to an abrupt and arbitrary end, leaving me with nothing, shook me. He seemed to notice and looked down on me kindly, and it was just that— his kindness—that made me believe it might be okay after all, that the old man's death could work to my advantage. Harry wouldn't have the attachment to Marianne Rasmussen that Aubrey must still retain; Harry would be unfettered by either the love or the hate that must still bind Aubrey after such a grand affair. If Aubrey Ash were to die soon, wouldn't everything be simpler for me? Harry would be pleased to hand over any letters or other papers in return for a small contribution to his cause. It would have to be small, unless I could drum up another grant or get a bigger advance or find a patron, and one of those might not be impossible—if I had the papers.

By the time I reached the front door, I'd measured the days ahead in the way they could pan out for me. If I had time to gain Aubrey's confidence, learn about his affair with Marianne, and get access to the papers, that would naturally be best. But if his death interrupted my plans—the man was nearly a hundred after all—a day or two with Harry should do the trick and I'd be skipping back home with my spoils. With all this in mind, I decided a visit to my publisher was in order, to get them thinking of that bigger advance. Maybe, I thought, in the years to come I would visit Harry once in a while, I'd trek to Toronto for business reasons, and each time drop in on him.

The oddest sound greeted my ears after the door closed behind me. I stood on the creaky stoop for some seconds trying to make out what it could be. It was an eerie, complaining sound, not unlike the squeak of the deteriorating wood under my feet when I shifted my weight, but lower, longer, sadder. Listening to it felt like an unpleasant out-of-body sensory experience, as if it were coming as much from me as from the world, as if I had sent out some turmoil inside me to be replicated in the world. Then I understood what it was: the wind had intensified while I'd been inside and was buffeting everything with almost equal force in every direction, and the trees, in their attempts not to buckle, were groaning.

# { 5 }

A WEEK LATER, irritated with everything that had trans-
pired and even more with what had not, I met Ryan Benson
for drinks and supper at a popular pub on Parliament Street
that he (irritatingly) called The Hop. Nothing was going as
planned, and without protecting my dignity, I admitted it
to him. My publisher hadn't gone for a bigger advance; they
would wait and see, and don't hold your breath in the meantime was the implication. I'd done a lot of waiting already
and I hadn't seen anything; I hadn't seen any evidence of
Marianne Rasmussen's letters, I hadn't seen Aubrey, not
even once since moving into that mouldy old mausoleum of
a house with its scary twin beside it. "In meeting you," I told
Ryan, "I'm skipping out on them. I'm not making their dinner tonight and I didn't even leave a note to let them know."

He laughed. "You're cooking for them?"

"Not only that, I'm buying the groceries. And the wine." I
knocked back another few ounces of my current glass.

"Oh dear, oh dear," he muttered.

"I haven't got anywhere," I moaned.

"You're being too timid," he said. "What about old Harry? I
thought you were going to wrap him around your little finger.
Hasn't that panned out?"

41

"He's the perfect gentleman and treats me with inevitable good humour, but I see him only once a day, when he comes downstairs for their dinner trays. First he takes Aubrey's up to him, and then he comes and gets his own. For breakfast and lunch, they make something or other up in their aerie. I don't know. Maybe they eat worms."

"Hah! You are annoyed."

"You would be too."

"I thought you'd do better. Why do you make them trays? If you didn't, they'd have to eat with you."

"Harry makes up the trays. I tried to prevent it. The first few days I set the dining room table. I even lit a fire; it was cool the first couple of days after I moved in. Harry smiled and said, 'How nice. It's good to see you're taking advantage of your rooms.' I'd set the table for two and made a tray for Aubrey. Harry took it upstairs—absolutely refused to let me do it—and when he came down to find me standing behind my chair, waiting for him—and it must have looked inviting, the chandelier lighting the room all shimmery, the fire glowing, the table set with their good dishes and silver, and I'd outdone myself on the meal—he, as I said, got a tray for himself, took his place setting and a helping of everything, including wine I might add, and without a word turned and left me."

"Poor you!" Ryan said.

"That's the only time I see him. Every evening he brings down their dirty dishes and takes up their food, and he hardly ever speaks."

"And you do the dishes too." He put a hand to his mouth as if even uttering those words was horrifying to him.

I have to say, before the end of my evening with Ryan I was glad to hear he was going away for a few months, although my contentment fled when I learned why. He'd been given a travel grant to write in Paris. "You?" I said, not bothering to hide my astonishment. Needless to say, he enjoyed the moment. "Everyone's a writer," I muttered, and ordered another glass of house red.

---

On the way back to the brothers' house, I remembered a few moments from the week before, when we rode the streetcar to Cabbagetown. At one point in our conversation, Ryan's phone had pinged. He'd excused himself with a finger. The streetcar stopped then, as if it had not ever expected to have to do that, and while we righted ourselves a drab old man with a scowl and a cane dragged himself up the steps and presented his pass to the driver. His glance swept across the row of single seats, implying that every one of us sitting there had taken them illegitimately. I started to stand, but he knocked his cane at the foot of the seat next to me, and the girl sitting there jumped up. That was all, or it would have been all, except that across the aisle two women in pink T-shirts giggled almost uncontrollably over something one whispered to the other. Their heads touched; their black curls blended. I couldn't help smiling at them; it seemed a harmless bit of across-the-aisle camaraderie to share their amusement. The old man leaned his cane against my knee. I felt it was deliberate. To pay me back for a momentary enjoyment. A small thing you might well say, one of those trivial rubs of one person against another. I sat quietly, resentfully, with the cane against my knee, knowing full well the old guy was daring me to move it. What made the incident memorable, I suppose, was the way Ryan reached down and handed the cane back to its owner. He did it in such a debonair way the old man only harrumphed.

My situation, although I hadn't made any progress towards my goal, wasn't as dreadful as I'd made out to Ryan; I was disappointed and stymied but I still had hope, and I returned that night thinking he'd been right about one thing: I had been too timid, too accepting of the regime the men had imposed. From the first—and I hardly knew how it had happened, given my plans—they'd had it all their way. Arriving at noon the first day, as requested, I'd handed over the month's exorbitant rent. But before that, you may picture me setting the groceries I'd just purchased on the kitchen counter. Oh yes, Harry had made an appearance on that occasion. He poked through the groceries to see what I'd bought. And I hadn't got a receipt for the rent. I had expected one, I needed one; I was living on a grant after all and would have to account for my expenses. But it wasn't offered and I still hadn't got up the nerve to ask for it. I hadn't wanted any friction between us, hadn't wanted to feed them any vinegar when honey should be more effective. Later I came to wonder if they didn't want to give me a piece of paper with Aubrey's signature on it; maybe they thought his signature would be valuable, and even Harry's, because of that, would be worth something.

———————

My first few days in the house on Ontario Street, I put Harry's behaviour down to pride or even his reputed shyness. I kept an eye out for his comings and goings and there were none. I didn't see him leave the house once, and no one ever visited, so no wonder he was reticent about sharing his time with me. When he got used to me, I posited, he would see that we could be friendly without any harm to his integrity. And there was a charm about the place, in the spacious old rooms with their darkly varnished, highly polished woodwork. The kitchen and bathroom were functional, although working in them was like being transported back a few decades. The sofa in the living room was long enough to allow me to sleep in compromised but not no comfort, and the back garden was, as we used to say, to die for. Tackling it, I'd had to be careful not to make that literal. At the back of the space was a tightly boarded fence heavily hung with vines that reached over my head. A few cedars grew higher than that, but apparently nothing was high enough that alley passersby couldn't toss their garbage over from time to time, and over the fence and hedge, over the years, they had. Soggy bags of old doggy shit were nothing compared to the syringes and condoms. With rubber gloves I found under the sink and a broom and dustpan, and with shears to cut through the vines and hack down the hardier weeds, I cleared a section of the brick floor large enough to hold a little high table I brought out from the living room and one of the kitchen chairs. And there I sat for a portion of every day that it didn't rain, in the tangled, hidden garden, surrounded by sweet-smelling cedars and the various greens of moss and hostas, ferns and other ground covers I couldn't identify but could love. The garden was enchanting, it was my secret refuge, and while I sat there I seldom heard anyone pass in the alley and I never saw anyone look down at me from above. I thought I might, if such seclusion continued, try a little sunbathing around noon, when the beams could find me through the branches.

It was while I was feeling blessedly alone in the garden, with my laptop open but unused, actually gone black in front of me, that Marianne Rasmussen came to me again and brought me an eerie calmness and rightness of being. My friends had worried about me in the past two years. First they'd expressed their concern that I wasn't getting over my divorce, and when their interest in that waned—or I stopped looking like a Mack truck had hit me—they fretted over what they called my obsession with Marianne. They didn't understand. I was feeling my way. It wasn't anything I could explain to them. Something in her being as well as in her poetry met something inside me, that's how it was, and I started writing about her. First it was articles, then a book of essays, and now I was after the biography. It wasn't mere personal ambition that drove me. It was a restlessness, a longing. She was ahead of me, she and her poems, and part of me was there too, beyond myself.

Now, in the garden, where the ferns whispered to me in a language I could almost understand, I had my justification for thinking I could change my life. Here she was, in the patchy light, in the soft, warm air. She had come to watch over me, she was looking out for me, and wished me well. Like a wise sister, she encouraged me, first to daydream happily, somnolently, helplessly, in the filtered sunlight under the trees and hanging vines, and then to hit the keyboard and write.

I did not actually write, sitting there in the garden, but it was almost as good to feel that I soon would. Any day now I would begin because Marianne was with me. Oh it was lovely sitting there, in the green and glowing light of the best of summer, believing I would one day soon begin to work as she had worked, at the highest of human endeavours, the making of art. For it was to be a very literary biography. I was going to write a biography the way the best critics wrote criticism—in a quest to find a key. I loved the early book reviews of intelligent young reviewers, the reviews they wrote before they thought they knew the answers, when they searched all the fiction or poetry they encountered for the same thing I longed to find, and when they sometimes seemed at the edge of discovering it.

Once in a while in my ruminations the more practical side of my nature asserted itself with its more mundane concerns. It wasn't just for my own personal satisfaction or Marianne Rasmussen's reputation that I needed to write the biography and it needed to be good. It wasn't even a certain need I had to "show people" that I could write something fine. I had no other abilities besides editing and writing. I was on my own now, no supportive spouse to back me up, financially or emotionally, if I failed. I tried not to think about that. In the garden I didn't need to think about it; that was the wonderful thing. In the garden I felt myself on the cusp of accomplishment. Teetering there.

The great secret—that only I had divined—was the crucial importance of the affair Rasmussen had with Ash. Ryan Benson had found it intriguing, but I was the one who had established, through painstaking research into places and dates, that Aubrey was indisputably the lover at the heart of what I called the Flesh Poems, those lyrics that were so daring and so explicit they could literally stop you breathing. They had certainly made the reviewers of the time gasp. In those days, the same words that were said out loud weren't countenanced in print. Words were etched into paper in those days; maybe that's why they seemed to frighten people more.

A lesser poet than Marianne Rasmussen would have quailed at the critics' damning response to her work, but she didn't apologize for writing what she wanted to write. She used their narrowness to make her stronger. But imagine being the lover and reading lines and erotic images you knew were about you. The old story about the two of them dancing at the abbey came to me, and I glimpsed them in the hazy distance where the past occurs: Marianne and Aubrey, in their prime, slow dancing on the abbey lawn. I almost caught her face lifted to the moonlight. I knew what it would look like: ecstatic, in the saturated moment. But I didn't see her face. She skimmed past me into deep shadow, vanished just in time.

---

People lead such closed lives. Here I was living with two men, and they shared almost nothing with me. I was getting to know their culinary preferences and little else. Every day I quizzed Harry as he brushed by me, never engaging in any real conversation. Once I caught myself trotting along beside him as he walked out of the kitchen and down the hall towards the staircase. "How did you like the fish last night?" I found myself asking, when really I wanted to ask him how he lived, what he did with his hours, even where he spent them, whether with Aubrey or alone. "Was the rice too spicy?" I could not even imagine what either of them did all day.

"Delicious," he said, not stopping.

I stood at the bottom of the stairs and watched him reach the landing and turn to make his way up the next flight. He was getting handy with the tray; I didn't worry anymore that the quiche would end up on the carpet. In the meantime, watching him stride away from me daily, I was imperilling my dignity, what little I had left. Marianne wouldn't have followed him like a Pomeranian eager for a look. How I wished I had known her. No, that isn't true. I feared the worst would have happened if I'd had the chance to meet her. I was too much in awe; she would have squelched me. It would have been like meeting Virginia Woolf and being tongue-tied because of stupidly worrying about using the wrong fork or speaking above a murmur or revealing you couldn't read Greek. The thought of it would have sent me skittering to a real room of my own. The person I would most liked to have met was Marianne's husband. My friends thought I was nuts when I told them I was going to his funeral. "You've never met the man. You have no connection with him or her or their family." I flew to Vancouver, crashed the ceremony. I remember hoping the other mourners would wonder who I was—you know, the mystery woman who turns up, walks in late looking as if she should be trailing a long black veil.

I had an interesting chat with a cousin of the husband, which in the end made the journey worthwhile. It came about when I tripped on the way out of the chapel and she caught my elbow and kept me from falling. She told me Marianne had ruined Irv's life. She said Marianne had several times threatened to leave him and he'd always begged her to remain, or in the case of her affair with Ash, I suppose he had begged her to come back. I thought that decent of him; I had done the same when my husband left me. It was a few months before my divorce that I went to Irv's funeral, which was why my friends thought I was crazy; it was in their minds one more instance of out-of-control behaviour. Another was my plan (not acted on) to stalk the other woman, my husband's other woman. I wondered if Irv had ever considered doing that, if there was any chance he had spied on Marianne and Aubrey, if he might have followed her to Toronto and discovered where she went. I still believe he might have loitered around the Ontario Street house before its twin had the No Loitering sign posted on its door. It is sad to think of him lurking there under the restless elms.

"She lied to him, you know," the cousin said. "Day after day, living with him, sleeping with him, she lied to his face. Who could he trust after that?"

Well said, I might have said, having myself weathered the brunt of a similar pernicious assault, but instead I told the cousin, "You look like him." There had been a large photo of Irv over the coffin.

"Maybe a family resemblance," she said. Her lips twisted and I thought it was for his pain, for the hurt Marianne had caused. My own eyes smarted at the sight. She was wearing the oddest hat though. I mean, nobody wears hats anymore unless it's twenty below, or maybe a black tam if you need to look French. It was pink, what they used to call shocking pink, and made of artificial feathers that trembled with her slightest movements. I remember telling my friends about it as if to prove I wasn't the only weird one at the funeral.

The ceremony and interment were held in Burnaby. I had a huge taxi bill each way and lost both receipts. I remember riding back to the hotel that day and seeing nothing out the windows of the cab because of a thought that came to me as I waved goodbye to the cousin. Could the poems have been even more brilliant if Marianne had left Irv? For good? And would there have been more of them, simply because she would have lived alone, unencumbered with any consideration for the rights of a mate to some of her time and energy? It was the first glimmer I'd had that being dumped might not be such a bad thing. For Irv, poor fellow, desertion would have been catastrophic, but it was not necessarily the case for me. If I spent the rest of my life alone, I could write and write. Without love in my life, I'd be free. I recall feeling disloyal to Irv in even considering it. The insight fled right away anyway, as if it had never occurred to me; I forgot all the thoughts I had that might have been good for me those days. It was more fun, if you can call it fun, to plan an elaborate surveillance of the woman my husband had preferred to me. My friends should have been relieved when my focus shifted from her to my "obsession" with Marianne. I hadn't heard much from my friends since I'd come to Toronto. Only the odd email came through telling me about their lives; I think they'd given up on me and mine.

---

While I dined alone each evening under the chandelier's shimmer, I pondered the conundrum the brothers were posing. I tried to imagine what they were doing, what they were saying, what they were thinking while I sat alone downstairs. I wondered if they ever talked about me, if they cared enough to wonder what I was doing and thinking. One night, with the feeling that I was treading water, more like a dog drowning than a human—I mean without knowing why, why I was struggling and not letting go—I went to the front door after dinner, opened it and stood looking out. I didn't step outside; I didn't want to go anywhere, just to reassure myself, I think, that anywhere was still out there.

---

Of course I knew what I had to do; that is, what I had to do with Aubrey. I'd known it from the start. I'd put off thinking about it because it involved a complete lie, but now that so much time had passed with no results, I saw it was the only way to accomplish my goal. I suppose I wanted corroboration that I wasn't completely out of line, so I emailed Ryan Benson and asked if what I contemplated doing might have been his plan all along. Beside himself with being more Parisian than the Parisians ("a *croissant* with my *café express* at the counter each morning"), he didn't mind admitting I was correct. Piqued by the rumours, he'd got interested in writing about Marianne Rasmussen, but he agreed that if he'd been able to reach Aubrey, he would have told him it was his biography he was writing. "As it is," he went on, "I'm all taken up with my Paris project, so you go ahead."

It would be difficult to put Ryan forward as a moral compass, but I understood I would have to "go ahead" in order to get Aubrey Ash to talk. A simple subterfuge, unethical but easy. I rehearsed what I would say. It would be a literary biography, linking his life to his works; I would say he was being hailed, out there in the aesthetic climate he'd left behind, as a hot one, as an underrated writer, although I wouldn't use that phrase. No missteps and no flattery. I'd be businesslike, and I was sure he would buy it, just as Ryan had been sure. But that didn't solve the problem of his brother.

When I contemplated Harry, always in his absence because in his presence I grew flustered, I longed for him to readopt that caressing tone of voice, that lounging-in-doorways style of our first two days. I pined for a revival of the daydream feeling I'd adored feeling the day I'd lingered, with him behind me, in the sunlight in the dining room, when it seemed he would—or had—come up behind me to embrace me. He was so different now from what he'd been you'd think I might have discounted the past, put the difference down to my own faulty memory, my own wishful thinking, but instead it was the present I deemed wrong. I didn't like his present mode at all, so when I thought about Harry, I thought to hell with the past, to hell with the way he was now. It was only the future that counted, and as long as I was in that house, I could affect the future. Couldn't I? Yes I could. I could reach Harry Ash. Marianne wouldn't have tiptoed around him. I wanted to live the way she'd lived—reckless, free. Even thinking about it gave me a thrill.

---

I found myself standing in the hall at the base of the stairs, looking up at the light that shone down to the second floor from the big room above, and it seemed to me that the light was calling me, the light was a force encouraging me. It felt natural to let the light draw me up the steps before I knew I would climb them, and I was surprised that I didn't float up silently. Quite the opposite. The old wood under the carpet runner crackled and cracked at every step. By the time I'd got halfway up the first flight my heart was racing and I had to stop to recover. There was no reason for fear, I reassured myself. I hadn't been forbidden access to Aubrey Ash; I had just been ignored. Well, rebuffed. By Harry, who was acting like a guard, now that I thought about it—as if Aubrey Ash needed protection from me.

I could see the second floor landing from where I stood, and it occurred to me that I hadn't been invited there either, where Harry lived. The light spilling down the stairwell stopped exerting any pull. I wavered. And when you waver, when you fail to take those steps you intended to take, the inevitable happens: someone else takes steps instead. So I heard someone crossing the floor above me, Aubrey's floor. I looked up, listening. I heard nothing more and saw nothing.

No one came to the head of the stairs or descended, but I imagined Harry's feet and legs and then the rest of him appearing above me. I imagined him stepping down and lightly taking my elbow when he reached me. It was so real, this feeling that he'd come down to meet me, that we would descend the stairs side by side, I thought he must, at this very same moment, be imagining it too. So I turned and walked as quickly and quietly as I could down to the main floor, and before I knew it, I was back in the kitchen where presumably I belonged. I stood for some minutes in the middle of the kitchen, focused on the cupid point of my elbow, where it seemed one of his fingers had rested while he led me down.

I went out to the garden and soaked up the green-scented warmth that trickled through the vegetation until it released me from myself. Soon I drifted into imagining Aubrey and Marianne, the two of them, not in the garden with me, or on the abbey lawn, but strolling hand in hand through the genteel city streets of an older Toronto. Early sixties. Black turtleneck for him, a chic shift dress for her, wrinkled in the right places, casually elegant like her dark bouffant hair, just the right cut for her cheekbones and ever undamaged by wind. No, wind could not harm her; she only looked more appealingly herself when rumpled. Aubrey would have been the same, an imposing man, easily attracting attention. I imagined them causing a stir on the sidewalks, trailing smoke and the musky scent of recent sex. I saw them stopping to admire their own reflections in the shop windows, laughing into each other's eyes.

What conversations they must have had, I thought. The content of the things they said to each other didn't come to me, but I heard the tenor of their dialogue thrum in the air around me and I knew I was sitting at the beating heart of the biography I was going to write. And Marianne was on my side. "Come along," she seemed to say, standing between me and the house, beckoning towards the door with a negligently held cigarette and exuding a sweaty lustiness I could almost smell through the smoke. She knew I longed to follow her wherever she led. She wanted to show me how she had lived on the outskirts of convention, and how it had changed her, made her into the enigma she became. She wanted to show me the truth she knew: poetry *is* sex. And here I was, in the garden of her lover. *Forgiveness like the soft underarm of the over forties.* That line came to me, from one of her Flesh Poems, and with it an idea. A lot of forgiveness would have been required of Irv afterwards, when the affair with Aubrey was over. Was she saying it was a weak thing? To forgive? Or maybe an endeavour best undertaken by the mature person, one whom sadness has aged to softness.

I opened my laptop; it had been sitting there for hours and the lid was almost too hot to touch. I really needed to get to work. The biography I was going to write was already written in my mind. I knew what it had to say; except for the details of her life, it was finished. I opened a new document and wrote her name. A fleck on the screen looked like an accent over the e at the end of Marianne, and I thought: Just so, a dash of real makes my fantasy exotic. I don't need to go to Paris; everything I need is here.

---

I came out of the washroom later that day, more confident than usual, having written my first few sentences, to find Harry Ash making up his trays, helping himself to the beef Wellington and mushroom sauce, the mashed potatoes, the green beans—I'd made them a real man's meal. He didn't hear me at the kitchen doorway and startled when he turned to take the first tray upstairs. He put on his slight affability while he walked towards me, that how-nice-to-see-you-I'd-forgotten-all-about-you act of his. I didn't move out of his way. This was not a thing I could do with calmness, this refusal to budge when I knew he wanted by, but I held my ground. It was high time to take a stand.

But there was a problem. The problem wasn't only that I couldn't speak, but that he didn't speak either. So we were stuck in the doorway; we were stuck there for what awkwardly came to seem a ridiculously long time. Were we each too stubborn to move? Or were we like a couple of magnets locked in perpetual suspense, not knowing whether we were attracting or repelling and unable to do either? I suppose the tray got heavy, or he finally understood we would freeze there forever if he had to depend on me to end the impasse, and he said my name. Just that, but I mean he said my mother's name. He said my mother's name and I'd forgotten that was the one I'd given him. For a terrifying moment I thought he'd mistaken me for her. I froze. I almost said, "She's dead." The expression on his face saved me; he looked so concerned I had to gather myself. I tried to speak but I could find no words. I had to look away, into the hall, over to the stairs. He was still holding the tray. It was weighing on me too. I stepped aside to let him pass and watched my hand trying to dismiss him, indicating he should go.

He didn't pass through; he stayed right where he was. The tray sagged a little. "Please," I said. But no, he wasn't going anywhere; he was waiting for me to explain myself.

My phone pinged. I couldn't believe my luck. Let off the hook, just when I felt most pressed, most obliged. Like rain after drought, manna from heaven, this diversion, exactly what I needed. "That will be my husband," I said, looking up again into Harry's face.

There was no way it would be my ex-husband sending me any kind of message at all. We had long ago finished with lawyers, which was the last step before being finished with each other. The last text I'd got from him said something like the several before had said: Don't embarrass yourself again.

Harry was looking at me as if I were imploding before his eyes. "I don't know why I said that," I told him. "The only messages I ever get are from my so-called service provider." When the damn thing pinged again I walked away.

# { 6 }

FINALLY I WENT OUT into the city. It was evening but still bright daylight; I rode a streetcar west for a while and then I walked for a long time until I came to a park. For half an hour or so I sat on one end of a bench while another solitary soul sat on the other. Later I found an outdoor café at the corner of an intersection. People were chatting, laughing. Strings of fairy lights tried to brighten the patio before it was really dark. I took a table and asked for a drink. It was early for self-pity, so I started watching a man, a definite alpha male who sat nearby, watched him kick back and check his phone, guessed how much more quickly he'd be waited on than I had been, and was correct in that. I listened while he ordered his drink and a late supper. He knew the menu in advance or didn't care what was on it. I could see he was full of energy, lightly kept in check. He was waiting for the something that was bound to happen to him.

I brooded over my drink, stroking the glass, aiming for a moody noir look. The evening was very warm. I was reminded of my mother. She'd pinned sweat shields into all her clothes, all summer long. She showed them to me, recommended them the year I turned thirteen. My armpits at that time had a new tinny smell I loved.

When people die we often say we've lost them, but I lost my mother before she died. I had not mourned her; maybe it was too soon to mourn—a matter of a few months after all—or maybe I never would. Our relationship (can you call it that, a mother–daughter *relationship*?) broke right after my marriage breakdown. Panic was her response to that failure. I knew why she was anxious and couldn't keep her anxiety out of her voice. She didn't trust me to look after myself. She wanted details, she wanted to hear the story, to be the one to commiserate, but even more to *know*, to know what was happening to me. So I refused her phone calls. I resisted, I refused. I wouldn't talk to her, not to explain myself or to reassure her.

A woman joined the man I was watching. She had his same kind of energy, had just worked out and showered; her hair, yanked up into a messy bun, was still damp. Tendrils curled at her neck the way they're supposed to curl. Something about her reminded me of the woman I had once contemplated stalking; Suzanne was her name. Possibly it was only the light scent of cologne or body shampoo hovering over our tables that made me think of Suzanne. I met her once in a restaurant washroom. It was completely accidental; she was coming out as I was going in. There was a second of eye contact. It wasn't her fault, of course, that my marriage had ended, but I did wish I could do her harm. Apparently she'd felt threatened by me; I was warned not to look at her like that again.

I had a second drink. By this time it was dark enough that the lights strung around us made some sense. I decided to focus on a younger guy sitting alone, lit in dapples at the far edge of the patio. He must be hungry, I thought, because he kept straightening his cutlery. Every time I looked over, he was shifting a fork or a knife, a minor adjustment and a whimsical enterprise on a wooden plank table. I wondered what my ex would think if I texted him and told him what I was doing. I could describe the neatness of the cutlery man. I could speculate on how that neatness would play out in a sexual encounter. I liked thinking about it and imagining his reaction. In my second adolescence (I could only hope this one would be shorter) I regretted the truncation of the first. If finding your true love is the developmental goal of those early years, it may still be unfortunate from the point of view of a lifetime to find him at seventeen.

I took my time walking home. The evening, as I said, was warm; everyone ambled, lulled by the soft, humid air. The street lamps lit the few small trees along the sidewalks, and I thought about cutlery man, sitting alone, sprinkled with phoney starshine. I thought about my ex-husband; I could see his figure half a block ahead of me, walking away from me as he had the last time I saw him. I thought about my book, the book I was going to write that was going to turn my life around. I thought about poetry. Secretly (as if anyone cared to know what I did), I'd begun writing some poetry of my own, not anything to speak of, not complete poems, just a few lines here and there while I sat in the garden. Scribbles. Anything that came to me, because everything that came to me in the garden had a touch of magic in it.

I strolled along until I reached a rougher area, but even there I wasn't accosted. Money was all beggars would want from me, and I didn't carry a purse but kept some cash ready in my pockets to hand out. A few times I was frightened by someone obviously psychotic or drug-deranged. I'm a coward when it comes to my physical safety, and the thought of dealing in any way with anyone unpredictable had me watching alertly and hastening over to the other side of the street if I saw someone suspicious. When the traffic got sparse, like other women walking alone, I held my phone to my face as if talking to a friend.

I was passing the drug dealers' park at Allen Gardens when it occurred to me that writers have always loved gardens. I wondered if I could put together a book about some of the famous ones, their favourite haunts, their little writing huts. I kept to the other side of the street, so the people in the park were only dark shapes under trees, but they must have affected me because I began to think what an unfair world it was where some had private havens while others had to congregate like shadows under public trees. Why did we all put up with it? It was a mystery to me why every expensive vehicle wasn't keyed, why every window in every expensively renovated home in Cabbagetown wasn't smashed; it was a mystery to me (as I trudged past them) why the poor respected the wealth and possessions of the well-to-do.

I was in an odd, unsettled mood, arriving, I won't say home, but back on Ontario Street. Almost a revolutionary mood. In some other world where I was young and strong I brandished a torch and thousands marched down the street with me, shouting that they weren't going to take it anymore. But that was stupid; they were, and I was, we were all going to take it, we were going to go on as if it was fine for us to live the way we did. Feeling that the house couldn't contain me in my current state, that I'd grown somehow larger than my usual self, fiercer even than Marianne Rasmussen—I might have been Dorothy Livesay, implacable and on the hunt for a Goliath—I walked straight through the kitchen without turning on any lights, stopping only to pour a glass of wine on the way. I left the door behind me open for the breath of barely cooler air that might waft in, stood on the back step and gulped down a bit of the benevolence or whatever it was drink bestowed that nothing else did. We were far enough from a streetlamp that I waited there for my eyes to find my table and chair. I heard a noise, thought it might be a raccoon, and prepared to retreat. In any battle between me and a raccoon I would let the fiercest win. Then my eyes got more accustomed to the dark and I ran into a tree. So to speak. I saw Harry sitting in my chair. My glass slipped from my fingers and shattered with a sensational bright clatter on the bricks below. A dark puddle, dark as blood, ran over the bricks almost to Harry's feet. I couldn't think what to do. I could see the glinting shards and the dark stain on the bricks, the wine already soaked in, and I thought: broom and dustpan, pail and water, but I did nothing.

"Leave it," Harry said.

I saw that he'd brought out a second chair from the kitchen. I stepped over the mess with the feeling that the only way to make things right would be to turn time back and make the glass whole again. The same anxiety—I recognized it immediately—had engulfed me many times in the weeks before my divorce. I couldn't think why it should attack me now, at the sight of this man simply sitting in his garden, this feeling that something had gone irremediably wrong.

Harry reached out as soon as I sat down and touched my cheek. "What are you up to, my dear?" he said.

Oh dear, that my dear, was it designed to effect a response? A flood, a bent-over, head-on-knees, heart-on-ground, old-timey bawl? I thought it was, yet in spite of thinking so, I felt the heave, the halt, the longing to let go. I could imagine what would ensue. He wouldn't touch me again, he'd sit tight waiting for the sobbing to end, waiting for the stillness to come back into the dark garden. And when I sat up again, and only hiccups were left, and I could look around at the shadows, and my ears and eyes could take in the flutters of leaves and dim dabs of light on twigs and vines, and I could smell the earth and the vegetation, and the hiccups ended, he would hand me a Kleenex, and I would wipe my face and blow my nose. And then I would tell him the truth—after apologizing, the way you do when you've regurgitated a gutful of emotion in front of a person who has no idea why you're doing it. He would wait for that truth, sure it would come. There is such intimacy in talking quietly in a small garden on a dark night, my words would seem to be taken up by the moss and the leaves; yes, it would be easy and natural, after crying, to tell the truth. And there he was, so sympathetic. Yet another Harry? A different Harry? I would say something along the lines of, "I haven't cried like that before, ever. I didn't know it was in me. I guess I'm a bit of a mess." But how tedious to go on, to explain a husband of many years who'd walked away, a mother who'd died, an obsession with a dead poet that had so taken hold it had eventually alienated old friends, an isolation that now seemed curable only by the writing of one book. And that book was so all-important to me, I don't believe even if I had cried in front of him, I would have given up my plan. My body would have slowly calmed itself, slowly recuperated from the assault of those overwhelming feelings that really I couldn't have explained, and as it settled back to its normal state, I would have remembered my plan. I would have pulled myself together. So although my eyes brimmed and my throat burned, I held back. I didn't cry.

"You must wonder why I'm here," I said in a voice that conveyed some of the self-assurance I hoped to convey, and I peered at last through the darkness into what I could see of his face. Then came the biggest surprise of the night. Harry was crying. I blinked, thinking I'd imagined this outrage, this violation of male pride, but when I came closer, I found it was true. He was out-and-out crying. "What is it? What's wrong?" I asked, but before he could answer, the enormity of what it must be crashed down on me. "It isn't Aubrey? He didn't—" I couldn't even say the word die. "Oh God," I wailed. "I've wasted so much time."

Naturally, those were words I would have taken back if I could. What would he think? What did he think? I couldn't tell; I couldn't read his face in the dark. My outburst—a shameless, selfish revelation if there ever was one—should have provoked dismay if not disdain, but Harry's response, if I could ascertain it at all, baffled me. Again it appeared his sympathy was entirely with me. He nodded and said, "I know."

I glanced up to the top of the house, where Aubrey's window was, the one over the round, book-laden table. I could barely make out the frame against the brick wall and a slight black glare from the pane, but it held me, staring, so I was looking there when Harry said, "But it's not Aubrey. You don't need to worry about that. He's only failing. He's not dead."

Even in the dark it would have been hard to conceal my feelings if I hadn't kept turned away from him, because anger was how I responded. You might say rage. I could have decked the man for letting me think all my hopes had come to an end, not to mention for setting me up to reveal my shallowness. But then I thought a failing Aubrey could be as bad for my purpose as a dead one. If they hadn't let me near him when he was as hale as any ninety-nine-year-old could be, how did I think I could quiz him when he was fucking failing?

It felt as if I'd been through way too much, and these brothers, these unknowable, inimitable brothers, were to blame. Old men. I'd had enough of them. And they were

64

everywhere, everywhere I turned. On the streetcar earlier that evening I'd encountered a bitter old man. I wondered if I'd met him before, if he was the same belligerent old fellow who'd laid his cane against my knee. Because this old man had a cane too. He'd left it deliberately out in the aisle and a girl had tripped over it. Of course he was the same old man. Thinking of it made me angrier than ever. But then I remembered who boarded right after that, a tiny old woman dressed in most of the colours clothing comes in, from her two-toned shoes and striped tights to the ribbons at the ends of her bright white Pippi Longstocking braids. She stepped over the cane and sat down beside me. Eyeing the old fellow severely, she said, "He's lucky I didn't hit him. I feel like hitting someone tonight."

I said, "I often feel like that myself."

Cheered by the thought of her and our conversation, I composed my face and turned back to Harry and said I was both relieved and sorry.

"He'll die, when he's good and ready," Harry said. "And not until. Don't waste your tears on him. He's been an asshole all his life. For some reason I believed you were a widow."

That was a swerve I hadn't expected. All I could say was, "What?"

"I guess I was I wrong."

"I'm divorced."

"I'm sorry."

"Oh it was two years ago. I'm over it, you know."

"I never married," he said.

I had no idea why he was talking to me like this, but it seemed best to go along with him and try to find out. "You were saved from that dire fate?" I asked, hoping to lighten the conversation.

65

"You might think of it that way." He sounded ineffably sad. I had a strange urge to wipe tears from my face, but there were no tears. "It's a good thing we die," he said. "Life would be unbearable if you had to think it would go on forever."

We sat for some time contemplating that statement in the beautiful tangled garden with the trees murmuring above us and all quiet otherwise around us. Although I was coming to understand that I didn't know him at all, I had the feeling we'd become friends, Harry and I. In a matter of minutes, almost magically, we had connected. His voice had reached out to me, in the confiding way the voices of friends do in situations such as this, two people sitting quietly late at night in the dark. He started talking about Aubrey, and I was certain then that we'd made a breakthrough, a truce had been declared. He'd wanted one too. As much as I had, he'd wanted the guardrails to come down. I didn't see for a while that he was still speaking of death and of Aubrey's inevitable demise. "He sleeps almost all the time, dozes more than sleeps, off and on all day. He doesn't eat all I put on his tray. I could give him less. I'm waiting for the day he refuses food. They say that's how it happens when you're old and your body won't die for you."

I thought of bringing up the topic of a biography—surely it would have been an appropriate moment—but before I could introduce it, he segued into talking about his youth, describing what Toronto was like back in the days when his father worked for the exhibition board as something of a bigwig, I gathered, and the summers were spent either at the grandstands and rides or at their Muskoka cottage and sailing on either Georgian Bay or Lake Ontario. How they'd come down in the world, I thought. "Was this your family home?" I asked.

"This? No."

The no had been an unconscious scoff, and I suppose I reacted, jerked and moved away from him. I had been raised in a house not half as big and gracious as this one, and clearly for him it was not anything so grand. Again, his response to my reaction was sympathetic. He put his hand out, not to touch me, but to be nearer, to lie on the table close to mine. "When you get old," he said, "time collapses every once in a while, and it seems all that was yesterday." I could feel him smile and his body relax. "You get sentimental. Tears come easily to an old guy's eyes."

I said he didn't seem old to me.

"I forget my age. Maybe it'll only really come home to me when Aubrey goes. Nothing like feeling young when your way older brother's still kicking."

"And you look after him."

"No, I don't. I take him food. I keep his place clean enough. That's it. If he needs more, if he ever gets to need more, he'll be out the door."

I wondered if that were true.

"He knows it too," Harry said.

He sat back in his chair and stretched his legs out in front of him, to my side of the table. I looked at the inch that separated our denim knees and felt such an incredibly luscious pang of desire I couldn't move. What did Marianne write? *A ripe cantaloupe just fell inside me!* So there I sat, smiling to myself about my weighty cantaloupe.

Some time passed, could have been whole minutes. Neither Harry nor I moved. I wondered why I wanted him when I was so full of myself. And when the waiting got unbearable, because I did want him, and yet the thought of moving towards him terrified me, I started asking myself questions, simply to divert my own attention from the inanity of sitting there with that decorous inch separating us. Why had he decided to tell me things about himself? Was this supposed to be an exchange? I'll reveal me, and then it will be your turn? I began to expect another swerve, and while I waited for it, I swerved too. I reminded myself of all the days I'd cooked for him and his brother and got nothing in return, not a smile, not a word. I had to think this could be a trap laid for me, to make me tell exactly what he'd asked when I walked into the garden. What are you up to, my dear? So I went on my guard again, yes, all over again. But at the same time, completely contradictorily, I longed to open up and ask him if he suspected the truth about me. It would have been a great relief to get things clear between us.

I grew resentful. There we sat, in the silvery shadows thrown down by half a moon. An inch between us. The air lifted and sank around us like a sigh. How much more voluptuous it would feel on bare skin. I knew what Aubrey and Marianne would have done. Against the house wall. On the brick floor. In the dubious ferns. Anywhere, everywhere. Why shouldn't we? God, live a few minutes—or a few hours—why not be greedy?—as if we were Aubrey and Marianne. And then I thought, I could ask him to dance with me.

"I don't understand you," he said abruptly.

I didn't know what to say. Neither of us moved so much as our little fingers, lying near enough to touch on the table. It seemed darker; a cloud must have passed over the moon. "I don't understand *you*," I said finally.

"There we are." He stood up. I stood up. He ushered me to the door. Then he changed course again. "Do you write at night?" he asked. The caress was back in his voice. "Will you go to your room now and write?"

I blinked up at him. He was examining me with a tender regard, like an old lover might, an old lover coming upon you after years have passed, finding himself almost overcome with fondness for you, or for the memory of you. Near tears—again—I babbled something about reading in the evenings, on my laptop, or in bed on my phone. "They say it's bad for you, the blue light or something, but I need to stop my brain. Whirr, whirr, you know. Only someone else's words can stop it." Now he looked amused, with a kind of pleased approbation that reminded me of the schoolboys who'd liked to tease me. It made a little spurt of boldness rise in me. "I like poetry at night," I said. "Do you know of Marianne Rasmussen? Do you know her work? She's wonderful, so piercing with her observations, yet somehow the fact that she makes them comforts me. Or I mean, makes me optimistic."

"Yes," Harry said. "I've read her. Aubrey has her books."

"I know some of her poems by heart," I said. "I love them so. It's poetry like a rollercoaster ride. You know she's going to bring you to the top and then thrillingly drop you—but there's also, always, a chance you could fly off, and it's that chance—that you could fly free—that keeps you reading her."

"Aubrey knew her. He knew her well."

My heart jumped into my mouth. I looked down before he could see my eyes widen. And there was the shattered wine glass, on the doorsill. He took my elbow; it was an electric touch. "I'm going to clean that up," he said.

"But I did it, it was my fault." And then I had to ask, "Did you know her too?" He still had hold of my elbow, and now bent over me at the doorway. I was thinking two things at once: how different a real touch was from an imagined, and that for sure he would kiss me. I wanted him to kiss me. And he came close, his face came close to mine, but he didn't kiss

69

me; instead he slowly shook his head. His lips were near my cheek. I stayed so still I began to feel paralyzed. I didn't know what he was doing to me.

"I suppose you'd like to ask him about her," he said.

His words buzzed in my ear and set it tingling. "Yes," I said.

"He was crazy about her. When he first moved in with me, she was all he could talk about, even though decades had passed since he'd seen the woman. He raved about her and about the way she treated him. But he doesn't talk about her anymore. He won't tell you anything."

"But please," I said, pulling back from him at last. "You could ask him for me."

"That would make him less likely to comply."

---

Harry walked with me through the kitchen, down the hall, and into my makeshift bedroom. I'd closed off the double doors to the dining room, and he hadn't entered the living room area since I'd come to the house, or not as far as I knew. My things were scattered on the furniture; I had no closet or drawers to keep them in, and I hadn't bothered to be neat. Now with him seeing my mess, it felt as if I'd lost some privacy I should have been more careful to maintain.

"Good night," he said.

"Does he have pictures of her?"

"What? Pictures? You mean photos? Maybe. I don't know what he has. Is that what you're up to? You're writing about her? Is that why you're here? For a book?"

The way he said book, he might have well said for a jog around the park, for a ride at the fair, for a sail on Georgian

Bay, something flimsy and temporal and meant for a day. Like a kiss in a doorway. Meaning nothing.

"I am here for a book," I said, and I gained strength from that partial truth. "But not about her. I want to write about Aubrey."

If I thought that would soften him or help me in any way, I could see I was wrong. He scowled. He turned his back on me and was gone.

I couldn't cry; I hadn't cried for two years and had perhaps lost the ability. I didn't even know why I wanted to cry, or why the feeling had started when I came to the open back door and saw Harry sitting there in the space I'd cleared in the garden. But that wasn't when tears threatened, was it? It must have been when he touched my cheek and asked, "What are you up to, my dear?"

Ah no. It was the broken glass, and wishing, as with all things broken, I could turn time back.

No, it was seeing him in my garden.

# { 7 }

HARRY CAME INTO the kitchen while I was unpacking groceries and said Aubrey wanted to talk to me. I flashed him a question with my eyes; he chose not to answer it.

"When?" I asked his back.

A nearly imperceptible shrug made him seem a younger man. "Now, or as soon as you're free."

He was brusque, so I deduced he wasn't happy that I'd been called, but I was sky-high. In my mind I was already in the aerie. "Just let me put these things in the fridge." He'd left and hadn't climbed back upstairs, I noticed, so either he was hovering in the hall or he'd gone into my room. I took some umbrage at that thought but I didn't need to fuss. I heard the front door open and close, and the key turn in the lock. They kept their doors locked, I'd noticed, even when at home. Well you would, living with the evil twin next door.

Too late, at least too late to question him, I began to wonder what was going on, why Harry had gone out when I hadn't seen him leave the house even once before, and why suddenly I'd been invited for an audience with the Great One. It could simply be that Harry had relayed the information that I was planning to write Aubrey's biography. I hoped it was that, but how could I be sure they meant well? Harry changed from day to day, and I had no way of knowing what Aubrey was thinking. I had no choice but to see him anyway; my whole reason for being in their house was to see him and talk to him and persuade him to talk to me.

So I climbed up to the aerie, where space and light fought with an atmosphere of claustrophobia. But whose claustrophobia was it? Aubrey's or mine? He was sitting in the same chair, in the same sweats he'd worn before, and he looked older, more sunk into himself, which I suppose makes sense if he really was failing, as Harry had said. Again he was wearing sunglasses and again he looked cool in them. It was incredible. He was a mess; his flesh hung from his bones; it was bruised in a hundred places. Nearly every inch of his old thinned skin was scraped and scarred and scabbed. He was mottled and wattled and he shook. All aquiver all the time. But he had a natural flair, an innate sense of style, as well as the old laid-back charm I thought at odds with the drama he seemed to like to incite. I was relieved to note that he appeared pleased to see me. I glanced at the table as I sat down in the chair across from him to see if any of the books had changed, and they had not, as far as I could ascertain. They were detective novels and thrillers, all paperbacks with dated, faded covers, written by authors anonymous to me; there was a Jack and a Dan and a Clarence. I guess they might have been different novels from before with the same authors and the same formulas and I wouldn't have been any the wiser, but the dust on the table hadn't shifted a bit and I was pretty sure if I lifted any one of them, I'd see a rectangle underneath that would prove it hadn't moved.

I asked him how he was faring through the heat of the last few days. The third floor, I should add, stifled all but the biographer impulse in me; it must have been as close to a

73

hundred degrees on the old Fahrenheit scale as Aubrey Ash was to a hundred years. "I believe you have a birthday on the horizon," I said before he'd had a chance to answer my first question. I heard my voice chirp in the way voices do when they're delivering good news to the elderly, that is if the speaker is too stupid to realize the old person is still human. One of Aubrey's eyebrows lifted above the Ray-Bans. My heart thumped so hard it hurt. How could I be such an idiot?

With a lazy intonation, watching me all the while from the far shore he liked to inhabit, he said, "Why fade these children of the spring? born but to smile and fall."

I continued to feel stupid.

"Blake. Do you read him? Read a line a day; it will bolster you for the slings and arrows. But I didn't haul you up here to talk about that." He paused. One of his hands had begun to tremble alarmingly, like an old vehicle in an old movie, starting up. While it shook, it grasped feebly at the nothing between us. We both stared at the hand, wondering what it wanted, until with effort he lowered it to his knee and turned his attention back to me. "I wanted to thank you for the meals. I should have done so before this, but—"

My phone pinged. I couldn't believe it. I was so stunned I didn't move. He regarded me with displeasure, as if I'd let a stranger into his house. "Answer it. I insist," he said.

I pulled my phone out of my pocket and remembered telling Harry I'd had a message from my ex. So revealing. He'd been concerned for me. I'd seen it in his face. And then in the garden, when I thought he was crying over Aubrey, could it be that he was upset over me? Over what I was doing here? What was I doing here? My thumb moved to delete the message that said I only had to call to collect my prize worth one-point-one million or something like that, and missed.

On the second try I successfully deleted the message, turned my phone off, and looked up at Aubrey. "Sorry."

"Hard to eliminate, aren't they?"

"Yes."

"They say they'll last forever, out in the ether somewhere. Emails too. Indelible, indestructible words. Not like the old days when we wrote on paper."

Footfalls on the stairs interrupted us again, just when I was trying to grasp his meaning. Harry appeared at the top of the flight and dragged a chair up to sit with us. I wondered where he had gone in the ten minutes he'd been missing. As I mentioned before, it was the first time I'd known him to leave the house.

"You weren't gone long," Aubrey said to him. "I was in the middle of thanking this lady for her cooking," He'd settled back in his chair and appealed to Harry in a chummy way. "The way to a man's heart, as you know." Something new there, an undercurrent, and it happened so quickly, I could hardly believe the change. He seemed to be insinuating I'd been trying it on with Harry—and insulting both of us at the same time. Yes, Aubrey had perked right up. He turned to me. "I hope you're not going to leave us in the lurch again, the way you did last night, taking off without feeding us or telling us you were going."

"Well," I said, "I don't think I'm your servant, and if I were, I'd still deserve a night off once in a while."

"A cold supper would be acceptable. You could prepare it before you go out gallivanting of an evening."

I laughed at that, though a bit helplessly, and Harry laughed too. "He's trying to say we appreciate you," he said.

I couldn't read Harry's face through his mask of good-humoured politeness. Impossible to tell whose side he was on, mine or Aubrey's. I still had the impression they had banded together to get something from me, something more than meals, and I decided it might be to my advantage to coax them into my territory instead of being trapped in theirs. I said, "Aubrey, why don't you come down to the kitchen? We could have a lovely meal, the three of us. Or come on a day like this, when it's warm in the house but gorgeous in the back garden. I could set up a picnic for us there. It would do you good."

"When I leave this attic, I'll go feet first," was his annoyed response. "I've had my *picnics*."

The bitterness he displayed reminded me of his misery over the idea that I might sit in his garden and write a masterpiece. To change the subject, I asked if he read fiction anymore, or poetry. I couldn't keep my gaze from referring to the genre fiction on his table.

He exploded. "Poetry! There's been none written since Shakespeare!"

"Oh, come on," I said. "There was Blake, and Harry tells me you knew one of the most beautiful poets ever to write in the English language." I hadn't meant to say it! Had I been tricked into saying it?

"I don't know who you mean," Aubrey grumbled.

I turned to Harry but he wasn't going to help me out. He was examining the faded Persian rug on the floor beside the bed.

"I mean Marianne Rasmussen," I said boldly. But my voice shook.

Aubrey looked away, not towards anything, but just away from me and from Harry too. "That's enough," he said. "You tire me. You bore me. I can't natter on the way you can." He flapped his hand in dismissal.

When I reached the stairs, he called, "Wait! I do appreciate your cooking. I'll live longer with you here feeding me. I'd just about given up eating faced with Harry's suppers."

That was all the thanks I got, and I'd missed the opportunity to ask for a receipt for the rent I'd paid (I had decided Aubrey's signature would be more valuable than Harry's if only for impressing my publisher), and I'd been dismissed before I'd been able to tell Aubrey about my plan to write his biography, but I felt as if I'd gained something in the exchange. Well, I'd spoken to him at last, got a foot in that further door, so to speak, but really I had to put an end to this ridiculous role-playing. I was a published author, researching in order to write an important biography. And I was playing cook and housemaid to two old men. I had to face the fact that if I'd been a man, on the hunt for papers held by a woman, the balance of power would have been on my side. No one would have expected meals. I would only have had to persevere to eventually win.

---

I explained to Harry the next day that I would have to get access to Aubrey on a daily basis or I was wasting too much time.

"He'd like you to stay on longer."

"When the month is up? I can't afford to pay any more rent. Is that why he wasn't letting me see him? To drag out the time so I'd have to pay more? And I need a receipt, by the way." I rattled all that off before I could think better of it. Harry looked pained. He suggested that the shopping and cooking might do as a substitute for rent from now on. "And the cleaning, don't forget I'm doing that," I appended.

"Tomorrow's his birthday," he said; seldom had he said anything so morosely.

I had to laugh and he smiled sheepishly in response.

"We'll have to celebrate. It's a landmark," I said. "I'll make a cake, but I can't think of a gift. I mean, what do you give a man who's turned a hundred?"

Harry shrugged. "Tell him you're going to write his biography. You'll see. He'll like it."

If the thought of Aubrey's birthday made Harry miserable, the idea of the biography had him drooping like a perennial in a prairie heatwave. "It doesn't seem to give you any joy," I observed.

He shook his head. "Too complicated," he said, and then, "He's a real asshole, don't forget that."

———————————

Mid-afternoon the next day, we carried the cake and fixings upstairs together and found the great Aubrey Ash in fine fettle, standing, actually standing to greet us. (The tall tree.) He was dressed in a pressed shirt and trousers and was wearing the sunglasses as always, and I guess that was a good thing for the protection of his old eyes, since his head had poked into a shaft of sunlight. The light was making little prisms of the transparent strands that stuck out from his skull; I was reminded of a novelty lamp of my childhood. So we began, gaily. He even exclaimed at the cake, which I had decorated only with his name, both names I should say, as if for a public event, though it was just the three of us who would see it. He loved that too, Aubrey Ash in blue icing, just barely fitting across the surface.

78

"She has another gift for you," Harry said.

Aubrey wasn't the only one who started at Harry's words, or rather at the way he'd said them. It seemed another meaning might be construed if anyone cared to look under that rock. We chose to ignore it.

"Another gift," Aubrey said, smiling to himself as if musing on a completely new and highly acceptable concept.

"I suppose what Harry is referring to is what I want to write. What I plan to write." I paused for breath before I stumbled over myself; in spite of recent practice, I still wasn't a good liar. "That is, I would like to write your biography."

He did not seem surprised. "So that's what you're up to," he said, and shook his great head and glanced at Harry, as if to say, Isn't she cute?

"I mean a literary biography. I feel it's time for a . . . " I'd been about to say reassessment, but God knows I didn't want to insult him. "A tribute," I said, and it seemed he liked that.

"You've studied my work?" he asked.

Luckily, I'd read everything he'd published; there were in fact only six slim trade paperbacks, so I was able to say with an air of authority that I knew his work well. A simple affirmation was hardly enough, however, to suit the occasion, so I scanned my critical vocabulary for some literary kudos with validity behind them: his vigour, his technical virtuosity, his sense of humour, the muscularity of his prose (that especially), and of course the humanity of his vision. He tossed his head as if to say praise didn't interest him, but it was obvious he was only pretending he wasn't preening. I tried to pretend I hadn't noticed. I do not know what Harry was pretending all this time.

"I suppose I've made a mark, in my small way," Aubrey said, and waited.

"Oh yes," I said. "You won't know this, but there's a lot of talk about you out there. Recently. People have been praising your work, saying—"

"Who?" he roared, sitting forward and gripping the arms of his chair. "Who's talking about me?" Excited in a way that seemed excessive, he once again tossed what remained of his mane, and I felt frightened.

"Well," I said. "Ryan Benson for one. I don't know if—"

"I know of him. Who else? What are they saying about me?"

I named a few others, and hoped they were high enough in the CanLit world to satisfy his ego. I was trying to think if there was someone international I could put forward, as that would of course mean more to him, when his gnarled old right hand waved between us and silenced me.

"I've been controversial," he said, settling back into his chair. "I knew I'd stir them up. I set out to do it. To do just that. And I did it with words, nothing but words. All a poor boy has in his arsenal. That's Bellow. I always attribute, and I never plagiarize, although..." He gazed over my head to stare at Harry. "I may steal." His shoulders went up and down in wheezy laughter.

His equanimity was restored.

I cut the cake, passed slices to the men and took one for myself. A few moments of silence along with the hit from the sugary confection soothed me and I dropped my guard, otherwise I wouldn't have been caught so unarmed when Aubrey began speaking of Marianne Rasmussen in his slow, mesmerizing way, and with something added, some tone or phrasing (I couldn't put my finger on exactly what it was) that suggested he had much to reveal if he wanted to go further, and which made me worry he might just possibly have seen right through me. But no, I consoled myself, shoring myself up while I listened, because his excitement and gratification had been genuine. He truly loved the idea of a tribute to his work. Well, I had to ask myself, who wouldn't?

"You mentioned Marianne Rasmussen the other day," was how he started. "An overrated poet. Always one to play what Bellow called 'the profundity game.' Women claimed her and pushed her above her worth, I'm afraid." He went on for some time in that vein, pretty much reversing the things I'd said about his writing to denigrate hers. Soon he was punctuating his comments with dramatic scowls and repeating his favourite insults (weak lines, feeble observations, feminine whining). He rubbed his chin and ran his hand through his wispy beard. I became concerned. He was getting worked up again. The old insouciance had fled as if it had never been. And then—it returned. I swear I saw a malevolent sparkle in his eyes, although they remained as obscured as ever behind the ever-present Ray-Bans so I could only have imagined it. He said, "Among my extensive files—correspondence, memorabilia—I have a nice nude photo of her you might like to see."

I'm sure I gulped and not soundlessly. He leaned back in his chair in an insolent pose and let me try to see past his sunglasses. "One of those photos that exposes more than a person knows, at the time. I'll show it to you one day. You'll see what a cunt she was."

I asked myself what I had done to deserve this.

"You don't need to take it personally," Aubrey said, clearly relishing that I did. We both looked to Harry. He'd walked away and was sitting on the edge of Aubrey's bed, staring into the convenient void before him.

I turned on Aubrey. "What could be worse, what could you do worse to a human, than reduce her to a body part? And someone so rounded . . . " Here I began to sputter. "So various and complete. To call her that is to—commit sacrilege."

"Dear lady," Aubrey said. "You are such a little virgin. I mean tiny, tiny, living all your life under a leaf. Have you never called a man a prick?"

I had more than once called my ex-husband a prick. The realization filled me with sudden glee. I had to laugh. I saw my own eyes then, reflected just for a second in his lenses.

"Silly word—prick—isn't it?" he said, still examining me. "One of irritation only, not promising any real ability to wound, whereas cunt has that guttural gravitas. Yes, a real force to be reckoned with is a cunt." He smiled on me and let that thought rest a moment, but he wasn't finished. "I discovered to my chagrin that Marianne was, at heart, a lesbian. Hence her popularity among the butch poets." He turned to Harry with an eyebrow raised in unfriendly inquiry.

Harry ignored him. I looked down at my cake with its three slices gone, its empty triangle of crumby plate, its thick, sweet layers, and its scrawled half a name.

"You should take our biographer out in the evenings, Harry. She shouldn't have to broach the city alone. Take her out touring, bar-hopping, whatever it is people do. What's the matter with you? Don't you know how to treat a woman?"

Harry picked up the cake; I piled the plates and forks; Aubrey laughed. With a bird of prey's grip, before I could walk away, he grabbed hold of my arm. "You said Ryan Benson is also interested in me?" he asked, and some underlying zing in his voice sent my nerves haywire. "Better watch out he doesn't get there before you."

I looked down at his old claw, fastened on my arm, and thought of Marianne. I could feel his force, that lust for life still coursing through him, spilling out of him, leaching from him to me, but my attraction sickened me. I was not as cruel as he; I couldn't fight him in his way, but I might have disconcerted him because I didn't try to rearrange my face or hide my feelings in any way as I thought about Marianne and how she had, just by leaving him, publicly and forever humiliated him.

## { 8 }

NINE A.M. I climbed back up to the aerie. Aubrey appeared
to be expecting me; he looked up as soon as I entered the
room. Interesting, I thought, how energy operates between
people, how my new confidence (you might even say com-
bativeness) immediately affected him. He actually waved to
me from across the room. I sped up, waving too, and then I
lurched. I mean in my mind I lurched; I didn't trip, I probably
didn't even slow down, but I thought of tripping and he saw
me think of it. When I looked up, he was smiling.

"Some questions, dear lady," he said cordially once I'd
settled down opposite him. "Most obvious, what makes you
qualified to write my biography?"

I told him about my articles and the published book of
essays.

"On me?" he asked.

I glanced at the window above us. I didn't know what kind
of day was happening out there and the sky didn't tell me.

"I suppose you came here with the book in mind. Is that
why you wanted to stay in the house? You could have told me,
you know. No need to be shy." He gave me his sitting-back,
approving-of-you smile. I will take you in, he seemed to say.

I can give absolution as easy as a smile. "Perhaps you've been seduced," he said, and the smile got broader.

My smile grew too as if to say I got the joke.

"I mean you might have been seduced by the idea of certain materials I may have squirrelled away, getting mouldy down in the basement. Old drafts of stories. Letters from literati. Things like that."

"Of course, I would love to see them. I've read all your fiction."

"So you said. Your own never went anywhere, did it?" He spoke gently, in the slow, lazy way he had, commiserating with me from behind the Ray-Bans. "Is that why you write the non stuff? Those that can, do. Those that can't, write biography?"

"In any genre, there are those writers who—"

"Rise above?" He nodded. "Exceed expectations?" He nodded again. "Think you're one of them? How much fiction have you published? How much poetry?"

"I have some publications," I said. "But we're supposed to be talking about you."

He laughed at that, and then I turned on my phone's voice recorder and we began day one.

---

The next morning I approached him more carefully. He observed my progress the whole way towards him and grinned when I sat down. I chose to smile briskly back at him. "Let's get started," I said, as if we were working on this project together.

He was slow in answering my questions but I didn't think he was consciously stalling. I figured he had something on his mind so I proceeded as if I hadn't noticed. While I

85

listened to his response to a softball query about his educa-
tion, I gazed around the room, not with any thought of seeing
anything I hadn't seen before, just to let him know I wasn't
anxious about the interview. Oh yes, I was a professional. I
was doing him a favour. I was repeating that reassurance to
myself when, out of the corner of my eye, I saw something
I had not seen before. A black-and-white photograph in a
severe silver frame, sitting on a shelf behind Aubrey. It was
propped against some books and half turned away from me,
so I couldn't see it clearly but I could make out the shape
in it; it was the shape of a woman. He was telling me a long
story about grade five, completely invented, I believe, involv-
ing the suggestive behaviour of his spinster teacher. I forced
myself to look away from the photograph, to look at him,
head to the side, my listening pose.

It wasn't until near the end of the session, after my eyes
had strayed a dozen times to the photo on the shelf, that he
addressed the elephant in the room, not by speaking of it,
but by turning away from me and reaching for the photograph. He was just able to take hold of it, and then he kept it
for some moments, gazing on it, before he handed it to me.
"Know who that is?"

I knew who it wasn't.

"Barbara Humphries. Beautiful, isn't she?"

Barbara Humphries had been a poet of some notoriety,
more famous for a few scandals she'd ignited than for her
work. But she was beautiful in the photograph, which was
tastefully supplied with shadows so it wasn't at all indecent
although she wore no clothes. It was a candid photo but curi-
ously formal, neutral. I thought that was because it was black
and white. Something about those grey limbs bleached the
life out of it.

"Did you just find it last night?" I asked. "I didn't notice it before."

"Things have a way of turning up," Aubrey said.

———————

Stepping from the shower that evening, I caught a glimpse of my body in the steamy mirror. I walked over and rubbed a clear space and thought about the photo of Marianne Rasmussen he'd told me about. It wouldn't be like the one of Barbara Humphries. I couldn't envision Marianne in all those artsy greys. It's true I'd imagined her under the moon's light, but that was silver and alive. Her photograph would be in colour and a lot more daring. It would carry the cachet of her whole being. I could not stop thinking what a photo like that could do for me and my book. It's a thing readers want to know, after all, not just how someone like Marianne Rasmussen thought and worked, not just how she lived, but how she was unclothed.

———————

Every morning I went upstairs and interviewed Aubrey Ash. Every morning I scanned the room for things that might turn up. And things did. Once I came to find the paperbacks piled at the back of the round table and an arc swiped into the dust. A manila file sat there, unopened, on the arc. "Did you bring me some documents?" I asked. I could adopt a very business-like voice when the situation asked for one.

"I plan to peruse them later, to see if any bits would interest you," he said.

"I'm sure I'll be interested in anything you can show me."

I didn't see the folder again. Other, subtler changes occurred nearly every day. Books came and went from the table, photographs appeared and disappeared, none of them of Marianne. I took the attitude that he was challenging me to feel at home in the space, so whenever a new photo appeared, I picked it up and asked him questions about it, displaying a polite interest. He seemed to enjoy those discussions. Sometimes he laughed out loud.

Patience, I told myself every morning as I set my phone to record. He spoke. I listened, or when I forgot to listen, the recorder did. His favourite topic, he being human, was himself. Sometimes he got quite witty about his favourite fragments from the past. He was not above self-deprecation if it paved the way to a boast. But there were always those *and yets*. "My best work was ignored. Not that I had trouble getting published wherever I wanted, but editors aren't what they used to be. Writers aren't generous, especially when it comes to awards. There's too much competition, and they're afraid if they raise somebody up, they'll lower themselves. A bunch of inflated egos; they don't see themselves as participating in literature. They're all individuals these days. It does me good to recognize I have nothing in common with the writers of today."

In spite of himself, there was one person who fascinated Aubrey more than he fascinated himself. All I had to do was keep him awake for fifteen minutes of rehashing his triumphs and his many instances of philistine neglect and we would come to Marianne. We would always come to Marianne. I could see him resisting, actually physically closing his lips and clenching his teeth against the urge. The poor man would fight it any way he could, with anything that might distract him; he would pick up one of his dusty paperbacks as if he might open it, or he'd pluck at the edges of his sleeve, or he'd gaze intently at a painting on the wall. There were several abstract paintings on the walls, all his own from an apparently tortured phase. I wondered if they'd been done during the days after Marianne left him. I wondered if I'd ever have the guts to ask him if they were from that time. Sometimes, on days when he hadn't begun by baiting me (he'd even started complaining about my cooking), looking at those paintings made me remember the real pain of betrayal.

---

My afternoons were different from my mornings. The day after Aubrey's birthday, watching me dump the rest of the cake into the garbage, Harry asked if he could join me for dinner. So at last we sat at the dining room table, under the chandelier, although its shimmer didn't do much to expand our mood. The next day he offered to act as my sous chef. "I'm making a salad," I told him. "It's too hot to cook." I got him to chop up some leftover roast chicken and boiled potatoes while I diced a shallot and sliced an avocado and made a dressing.

"What's that you're adding?" he wanted to know.

"Tarragon. It should be the fresh stuff but the dried will have to do. You had it in the cupboard. Probably it's old."

He said it wasn't old; he'd bought some herbs and spices in the last year, trying to up his cooking. "I watched some of those shows too," he said.

"I bet you're a good cook."

He only shook his head. I had the feeling I'd missed the point, but in a way it didn't matter; it was the best kind of harmony, the best antidote to his brother, having him beside me in the kitchen.

While he set up Aubrey's tray, he suggested we could have our supper in the garden. "Oh yes," I said, and I flushed all over with pleasure.

Watching him that evening, I liked what I saw more than ever: the white hair, combed back and still abundant, the big forehead, the trimmed beard, his face that seemed to tell exactly what he thought. He tapped his hand on the arm of his chair and I traced the blue under his freckled skin, thinking of the blood on its way back to his heart. I liked the soft hair on his arms and at the opening of his shirt. He was a man with just the right amount of hairiness. Harry-ness.

---

"You don't mention Marianne Rasmussen," Aubrey said one day when he couldn't wait to talk about her. "Yet you seem interested in her."

"I'm open to whatever you want to tell me," I said.

"Are you?" He laughed.

I blushed. He enjoyed that.

"She took her husband's name, you know, as women did in those days. She never expressed any inclination to drop it and become Mrs. Ash. Mrs. Aubrey Ash, as she would have been correctly addressed in those days. I think she liked her initials."

"M.R."

"You smile. I told you she was a lesbian. Or bi."

"Maybe androgyny was the key to her success."

90

"My turn to smile. You are such a little virgin. An angel on earth. I swear I see tiny, tiny gossamer wings sprouting from those sloping shoulders."

"Her writing is so confident," I said. "I wonder if she experienced her life through a double lens. You know, if she had a mind as male as it was female, if she had both and so life for her was richer than for most."

"Yeah, maybe that's the key."

He was laughing at me but I went on. "For women, agency is everything. In a society that wants to put you down—still—she cleared the ground. She freed her poetry." Freedom. That was why her words sang, I thought, that was why I read them like secrets I already half knew. "Something happened to her," I said. "Made her more assertive and elevated her poetry."

"I probably have scraps of drafts of hers around somewhere," he said. He sat farther back in his chair. After a few seconds he tired of looking at me and lifted his face to the window, where the sky was matte but blue. "Maybe letters too." His right hand lifted, trembled, and in an afterthought he smoothed his sparse hair back from his forehead. I looked away; I'd just remembered one of her poems, lines about taking a lover's picture down and leaving, to remember, the nail in the wall. I wondered if she might have seen a nail like that on a wall in the home she shared with Irv, one time when she returned.

I could sympathize with Aubrey, and often did, when I watched him trying to resist mentioning Marianne. I couldn't tell at those times if he was immersed in a pattern, trapped in his aging, memory-ridden brain, or if he was testing me, daring me to operate in the open. It ended each time in making me unhappy. Maybe that was enough.

The mornings drained me, but I kept going up to the aerie, I kept making recordings and taking notes, hoping if I could show myself to be sympathetic, if I could demonstrate a true biographical interest in him and everything he'd ever thought, he would give me the drafts and the letters he'd kept, and the photo, any photos, but especially the one he'd told me about. It was incontrovertible: that photo, maybe artistically blurred at a central point, or fig-leafed, would make my book. Maybe it could be the cover, if the marketers would dare that. A photograph of a beautiful woman with her legs spread open. Why not? It was Marianne. It was how her poems read. She wrote with everything open, including her heart.

---

Harry apologized for not asking if I would go out with him. We were sitting in the garden in the lovely gloaming, sipping our second glasses of wine. I hadn't ventured out in the evening again; I was too content where I was, and I said so. "Not to worry," I said, and lifted my glass in a salute.

Harry didn't respond in kind; he ran his hand through his hair and cleared his throat. I wondered how long it had been since he'd been out in the city for more than the ten minutes I knew about, which I now figured must have been at Aubrey's request. I didn't feel I could ask him about that incident; I'd found we had a better time when his brother wasn't mentioned.

"I haven't gone out much for years, just out of choice," he said. "I don't mean I'm a disillusioned old man in a world that's passed me by. I'm happy on my own. Temperament, that's all. But you can get to be too much of a hermit. One day you find it's difficult to imagine walking out the door, down the sidewalk, under the sky. Among other people."

"You don't have to explain."

He put up his hand to stop me. "I want to explain. I do go out for necessities, food for example, but I make it quick. And I get things delivered when I can. But I would like to go out with you. Until you came, it didn't seem a problem, or if it ever did, I was able to ignore it." He looked away from me and cleared his throat.

When he didn't say anything more, I said, "I would love to go out with you." When he nodded but didn't speak, I said, "God, isn't it beautiful here in the garden?"

"Yes it is," he said.

We watched the leaves tremble for a while in the dappled shadows, in the soft, warm summer breeze.

---

One morning Aubrey passed me a piece of paper as soon as I sat down. Wordlessly, I scanned the pencilled drawing on it. "Is it a map?" I asked finally.

"A landscape drawing. The bigger circles are trees; the smaller ones shrubs. The squiggles are some kind of perennial likely."

"And that's bricks in the middle? Is it your garden?"

"Someone's plan for the backyard, yes. I don't remember whose."

I set it down. I'd made it shake as noticeably as he had. I couldn't ask if it was hers. He knew I wouldn't dare. The answer meant too much. It would have been—I saw this immediately—the key to the door we kept locked between us. It would have been the end to lies.

---

Harry and I walked out of the house; I was relieved to see that he didn't display any trepidation. "Where to?" he asked.

"Show me around Cabbagetown," I said.

"Really?"

"Yeah. It's a great evening. Let's just stroll around."

It was a most summery evening and lots of people were out and about, strolling as we were, or working in their minuscule gardens, or giving their dogs the only exercise they were ever likely to get. Inappropriately, I thought, given his age, Harry took me east, away from the setting sun. I was letting him lead me, conscious as we went that we might have to turn around and return to the house if the pressure of being out in the world got to be too much for him. I had no way of knowing if he might get anxious and was preparing for that with a calm voice that floated in my brain, articulating nothing, just waiting in reserve, ready to save any situation.

Past Parliament Street we entered another residential area of old homes, some of them Victorian would-be mansions, some of them Lilliputian workers' cottages with long, low additions behind their dollhouse fronts. Here people walked more slowly or were tugged along by their dogs or children. Someone mowing a lawn provided us with the quintessential smell of summer, and we breathed it in gratefully. All the assurance and privilege of middle-class living, complete with third-floor decks for al fresco dining, bristled around us, but I didn't realize how much the

94

landscape had changed until I noticed that the people we met gleamed with the smooth skin and soft hair that spoke of spas, at least one shower a day, and better-than-adequate nutrition. I had grown used to the shopping area where we who could buy our groceries and wine and over-the-counter medications without blinking at the cost rubbed shoulders with a collection of the most disadvantaged people I'd ever encountered.

Eventually we ended up at a high wrought-iron fence that bordered a cemetery. "The Necropolis, the oldest burial ground in the city," Harry said. "It's a pleasant place to stroll. I believe Frank Graham is resting here somewhere."

I decided to ignore his comment, and he evidently appreciated that. I caught him smiling to himself.

"What an adorable little Gothic building," I said as we approached the entrance.

"Chapel and crematorium," he said.

I'd always considered the Gothic in any form to indicate a failure of the imagination, an easy, wanton waste of time, but I was charmed by the stone chapel's tiny, ornate beauty, its spires and peaks and curlicues, its drape of heavy, lush vines. "And the sky matches, filled with romantic pearly clouds and slanting light," I pointed out.

"Made for contemplation and regret," he said.

"Oh not regret."

He touched my arm and led me on.

"We can never attain this degree of greenness in Saskatchewan," I said, sighing because the green was so deep, so multihued and sunlight-speckled, so rich and thick and redolent of life and death all at once. "And look at the long shadows. There's a poem about being under a tree and the long shadow it casts. Louise Bogan. I wish I'd memorized it."

"You can find it on your Google when we get back," he said. "God, don't call it mine," I said. "The internet is dangerous." "Living is dangerous." He was smiling to himself again. I remembered he hadn't left his home for a long time. What a dear man he was, to come out like this with me.

The first grave we stopped at was Mary Helen's. She died in 1866, having survived life for approximately eight months. She shared her spot with Alexander, who lived eleven months, and Gertrude, who made it sixteen days over a year. "Living is dangerous," I repeated. Together we gazed over the grounds, at the stately fir trees and the generously branched deciduous trees, at the shadows thrown down on the thick grass, and the gravestones of all kinds and sizes (there were foursquare tombs that might have held Egyptians, and lowly slabs on the ground). "I love the lack of uniformity," I said. "Every grave is different from its neighbours, and they're scattered in such a homely, unorganized way for some reason I feel almost hopeful about mankind."

We ambled on, over the gravel paths and the lawns, through the shifting emerald light, remarking now and then on the inscriptions on stones or on the oddities we discovered, like one stone all ready for the wife to die, just the date left blank until she would lie beside her husband. Harry said it was quite a common convention. I shuddered, but then, at the thought that the future was inevitable for that woman, that she did not have to struggle towards it or against it, a weird sense of peace came over me. There is something about melancholy beauty that liberates a person from the ties of time, only temporarily, but what a respite it is. While I walked past the graves, under the tall trees, I felt innocent in a world that was innocent too. The way the low sun lit certain branches and not others seemed as important as the lives buried under the ground. I wasn't even bothered—as much as a biographer should be—by the many old, weathered gravestones, blank of names and dates, where the information that someone had once lived and loved—and been loved—had been blasted away. I remembered Ryan Benson teasing me about the concept of erasure, the last thing a biographer would want to hear, but in the Necropolis, it was possible to accept the lightness of being.

At the far side of the cemetery, a woman in shorts and a tight black T-shirt was digging with a spade, turning the earth at the base of a stone. A young man (her son, I decided) brought her a flat of bedding plants from the trunk of a car parked near the back gate. But my eyes were on her. She was at some risk, I thought, of digging too deep. Harry and I moved on, but I kept looking back, watching her until she straightened her back and glared at me. The word Nike was printed in white across her chest.

"In loving memory," the stones said. And "beloved." Son, daughter, father, mother, husband, wife, all beloved, at least for a while. Harry walked on ahead of me. I liked seeing him among the tree trunks, lit now and then by patches of sunlight. The Nike woman was still working, planting now. I didn't have a full view of her, and I didn't want her glaring at me again, so I shifted over to watch from behind a taller tombstone. She had to bend in half, with her substantial bottom in the air, to do the work. I imagined her grunting every time she stretched to plop another marigold or geranium into the spaded earth. I took out my phone and pretended I was photographing the grounds. I knew it was invasive of me, but I was just captivated by her. Such dedication and drive. Such speed and efficiency. And the bum in the air. There was a woman who knew what was important.

Harry waved to me but I ignored him. Her son was carrying two yellow lawn chairs to the grave, the plastic webbed kind. He had the bored look of a young man who doesn't sit on plastic lawn chairs, and I wondered if he would. Harry strolled up and touched my elbow. We took another path, in another direction. The air in the Necropolis was so cool it smelled cool, cool and deeply green. "The air here makes me sleepy," I said. It was a sleepiness a little like happiness, I thought. We stopped at a stone marking the resting place of a couple named Dickie. Harry said, "Mr. and Mrs. Dickie..."

Smirking, because I'd played that game too, long ago, I said, "And their son, Tricky." I leaned into him, nudging his arm with mine. We stayed for a few moments, smiling side by side.

After we'd walked on for a minute or so, he said, "Look." He pointed through branches, and I realized that the trees in front of us grew at a lower level than where we were standing. And there were more trees farther below.

"Listen," he said.

I heard traffic, a steady drone of vehicles.

"The Don Valley, now a highway. Come."

A few steps farther and the ravine was steep below us. We stood side by side, looking down. Now that I knew the highway was right there, I could see glimpses of cars and trucks whizzing by, somehow by their presence isolating us, making it seem as if we were the only two alive in the world, or the only two who knew it.

---

The helpful son was escorting an old woman to his mother when we returned to level ground. Slowly they crossed the lawn, through the shadows and the light, the old woman's feet barely lifting enough to top the grass. The mother waited with her hands on the back of one of the lawn chairs, as if to guide her son and his grandmother to the dock. The new flower bed blazed in many of the colours flowers come in. So that was the rush, that was the story, to make it pretty for the old woman.

On a plaque under a tall spruce tree, a rectangular slice of concrete stated one simple, bold word: MOTHER. It made me want a drink. When I discovered that Mary Jane Brown, beloved wife of William Black (what an exchange of names) died at age thirty-six, five months after her four-year-old son died, and nearby I learned that a girl of twenty was laid forever under an inscription that said, "If you love someone set them free," I said I'd had enough.

I looked up at Harry and saw that his face was white. "Are you all right?" I asked. He took hold of my arm. At the same time he held up his other hand. I turned to see what he was warding off. It was the gardener. She was making straight for us and she was mad. Imagine a short, tightly packed fire hydrant of a woman with a face about to burst. Nike stretched in white letters across the black T-shirt. She stayed wordless until she got right up to me, and then she said, "What the fuck do you think you're doing?"

I backed up. Harry, his hand still raised to try to stop her, said, "Hey."

"You've been spying on us."

"No," I said, weakly.

"What's wrong?" Harry asked her.

"She's been watching us since we got here. I think I know why."

Neither of us asked why. I think we were too stunned.

"You took pictures of us."

It was true; I couldn't deny it. I thought she hadn't seen me.

"Right here, right now, hand it over, hand your phone over. I'm deleting them."

"Come on now," Harry said. "Be reasonable."

"Fuck you," she said. "Now, the phone."

I took my phone out of my pocket and opened the photo app. "Two," I said. I showed her the two.

"Delete," she said.

I deleted them.

"Empty the trash."

My fingers shook. She grabbed the phone from me and did it herself.

"Mind your own fucking business from now on," she said. She had tiny, bright blue eyes encased in thick lids, both top and bottom. She did a good squint.

"Give her phone back," Harry said. She did, she gave it back. Her nose and upper lip were powdered with fine black dust. I'd have liked a picture of that.

On the way to the nearest tavern, he took my hand.

---

I woke from a dream feeling a heavy weight over me. I'd been walking in a cemetery and had come upon a grave I seemed to recognize. I knew before I could read the stone that it had my name on it. My husband, my ex-husband, silently appeared beside me, looking down on the grave with me, and I felt with aching certitude that he wanted me dead, that he had wanted me dead before he told me he was leaving me, and that even now his life would be better, smoother, happier if I ceased to exist.

I kicked off the sheet I had covering me, as if that would rid me of the oppression that had fallen on me. The weight I felt wasn't physical, yet my pulse surged, my breath caught before it could reach my chest. It seemed I'd put myself in mortal danger. Everyone was angry at me and I didn't know why.

# { 9 }

OF ALL THE WAYS to look at the world, the lens of paranoia is one that comes easily to me. Stories of bad service are always ready on my lips; waiters in restaurants, clerks in stores, I often suspect they've conspired to obstruct me. They don't want me in their establishments and won't tell me why, and they exchange glances when I complain.

I'd been ignored in the deli and left without buying the cheese I'd wanted. In a twee shop I was treated disdainfully in exchange for the opportunity to leave with three lemon tarts. I was wending my way through a small neighbourhood park, feeling that everyone was against me, when I looked a little farther than my navel and saw that the sky was crammed full of bulbous white clouds that looked like breasts. It was so unusual I took some pictures. There were hundreds of them hanging down, luminous, full, and pillowy. Who did I have to share this with? I was sorry that the first person I thought of was my ex. I could only conclude that I had my own traitor living inside me or I would never think of him again.

Before I put my phone away, I was assaulted by a sprinkler; water meant for the already lush grass sprayed the walkway and me. I came home wet and angry, sure that some park worker had set the sprinkler deliberately askew on purpose to ruin not just my day but everyone else's too.

"Write about it," Harry advised.

I didn't explain that suspicion of waiters and clerks and gardeners was not really the biggest subject occupying the back of my mind and that the anxiety that had set off my paranoia was about men. One of them him. Was he on my side or was he on Aubrey's? I was almost sure he sympathized with me, but did Aubrey have a hold of some kind over him? Even after our evening out, which had brought us closer, I still wondered if I could trust him. Also on my mind was the problem of whether or not I should reveal that I wasn't entirely trustworthy myself.

---

Out of the blue, or so it seemed to me, Harry said, "Once you're old it's time to start telling the truth."

I said, "Hah. Don't you believe it." Cynicism is also not foreign to my nature; I apologized for it, the way you do to sweep a subject under the rug. I did not like seeing his face looking so sincere.

He smiled, that looking-at-the-floor smile of his; in this case it was the brick floor of the back garden. We had just come out into the night, to the two chairs waiting for us there. He said, "No one is born a cynic."

"They're made, not born?"

"I doubt you'll find one under the age of four. Maybe five or six. And not because they're innocent until then, just because they don't fully distinguish themselves from the rest of the herd. They don't feel separate from others or from their environment, so they don't take bumps and bruises or even disasters personally."

"I suppose you're right. If a person perceives what happens as a slight or an otherwise intentional harm, it promotes..."

"The twist in vision that is cynicism."

I thought about my recurrent irritation at the rub of other people, the pinch of tight places, all the injustice and indignities. "You respond with the defences you can create," I said. "Cynicism is the bandage we wear to bind our wounds." Or was that paranoia? It was almost midnight by then and we were speaking metaphorically under the influence of dark shadows and red wine.

"And what cures them? Those wounds?" Harry asked.

I'd been thinking: Paranoia is the disease and cynicism is the cure, but then I fell back on Hell is other people, so I simply asked if he thought there was a cure.

He slipped his arm around my shoulders.

———————

One of the odd things about the brothers' house was that there was no way to see the street from inside. Windows at the back of the house revealed the garden, the few on the free side gave a view of the neighbouring double townhouse, only an arm's length away. The living room, now my bedroom, had a window, but it was made of opaque and bevelled glass that let in some light but allowed no vision of the outside world. One day I found myself opening the front door and standing there looking out, much as I had in my first weeks in the house.

I won't say I saw what I'm about to describe. I didn't see anything really, but I felt the past while I stood in that open doorway, as if it had walked up and thumbed its nose at me. People don't do that anymore. It's the middle finger now. The phrase was one of my mother's. She was not the one who appeared to me, although in a sense she stood beside me. It was as if she were remembering with me the day the young man who was to be my husband walked up the path to our door, how she and I stood side by side observing him. She'd guessed my excitement; afterwards she teased me about it and repeated what I'd said: "Oh Mum, isn't he cute?" Cute in those days (I was seventeen) meant I would have him, I would let him into the house.

Ex-husband is a word I could say quite glibly in conversation, but I could never think it with any equilibrium. I decided from now on to call him X, to picture him as X. He'd crossed out years of my life. Now I would do the same to him, make him virtually cease to exist. It was a good decision; it felt fine.

———————

I still visited Aubrey every morning for our interview. Some days he reprised his more engaging self and regaled me with stories of his interactions with other writers, always with an emphasis on their foibles. He could be quite amusing at their expense. Other times he went straight to their perfidies, their jealousy of him and his work, their idiotic dismissal of his worth. On the bad mornings he started with Marianne and all the reasons she'd been overrated. She had always received too much acclaim; she had sought it and got it, and her poems didn't merit it. "Read them yourself for Christ's sake," he said.

"I have read them," I said.

"If you think they're good, you've been fooled. Or you don't know how to read a line. You don't know what to pay attention to."

"That reminds me of Iris Murdoch," I said.

"Fucking hell." He wiped with annoyance at his face, as if he might have felt a tear on his cheek and wanted to annihilate the thing before I noticed it. "Well, go on, go on."

"She said the way to pay attention is to love."

"The way to pay attention is to love."

"Yes."

"She didn't say that. And she was regurgitating Simone Weil anyway. She said one should pay attention with love. You got the quote wrong."

"Aren't they the same thing?"

He waved me away, so I didn't find out if I had been right and they were the same thing, or if I was too dense, in his view, to understand the distinction he was making, if he really was making one and not just being an asshole.

---

Once he challenged me with this: "You don't mention Canadian writers. You don't quote them."

"And you don't either, or you talk about them, but not about their work, not in any serious way." Then I felt I should explain my own position. "I don't want to argue over them, haggle over their strengths, their merits, where they fall short. It would be like discussing your siblings with strangers. Afterwards you'd feel like a shit."

He still had charm when he wanted to use it. His voice dropped when he said, "Yes."

I glowed a little because he'd agreed with me.

"Yet you're so interested in me."

I looked around the aerie and found nowhere to land.

"And Marianne, of course. You sit up when the topic veers in her direction. If you had antennas, they'd quiver at her name. Someday I should show you some things I saved, things she left behind. I think I may have kept them." This was nothing but his usual slippery way of talking about his papers, and I looked around the room for distraction while he droned on. "If I did keep them, they'll be down in the basement somewhere, and likely ruined by the damp."

"Hey," I said, interrupting. "Was that painting always hanging there?" It was a particularly dark example of his work, a mostly grey painting with two great black slashes through it, crossing. An X of his own.

───────────────

My hour or two each day with Aubrey was always antagonistic in some sense, and I had to convince myself that somehow I was still working towards my goal, that one day soon I would break through his defences and get my reward. But my time with Harry, spent in the kitchen or the garden or on walks during gorgeous summer evenings, was marked with silly jokes in what seemed to be an increasingly attractive and funny external world. We chatted about nothing on those walks; it seemed it didn't matter what we said. Harry's good humour, good sense, and generous nature lifted my spirits; I think he shared my feeling that we went about like a pair of happy oddballs, almost carefree. But it might be that Harry saw our relationship in a more complicated way than I did, or that I had invested in believing it simple and good and all of itself, a package wrapped with a bow, belonging to its time and therefore capable of being set aside when its time was over.

"It's intellectual love Iris Murdoch was talking about," Aubrey grumbled one day.

"Like George Eliot," I said, with the reverence I could not help feeling and conveying when I said the name. "It's the kind of love that sees humble people as significant in the great pattern."

"Shee-it!" he said. "Humble people. Great pattern. There's neither. People are not humble, they're not great. All people are animals, that's all they are. There's no pattern, big or small, altruistic or mean. Don't parrot the inanities of the ancients. Christ, woman, grow up."

This wasn't the first time a man had told me to grow up. I realized I had a certain youthfulness that I didn't—maybe couldn't—keep down, but I didn't think I was immature. Maybe I was more in tune with my self than most. I felt like the same person who had read *The Bobbsey Twins*. I didn't believe I'd shed my previous iterations like dead skin, as we are constantly being told we do. I could find my six-year-old within me any time I looked for her. None of this was any of Aubrey's business, but I couldn't let him get away with talking about George Eliot that way.

"But it's the language that's old-fashioned," I said. "Not the thought. Eliot wanted to expand thinking, get people to sympathize with those different from themselves. Isn't that what fiction should do? Get us out of ourselves?"

I had been staring into space, delivering my defence of George Eliot as if she hovered nearby in a snit, requiring my support. When I looked at Aubrey again, he was shaking alarmingly, so alarmingly I was frightened he might explode—or have a heart attack in front of me. I half stood, thinking I should call Harry.

"Don't," he said. "Wait." He sank back, gasping, his hand flailing and grabbing at the air near his throat until he'd slowed his breathing. Then he said the most surprising thing ever to come out of him in my hearing, surprising because it was completely without rancour. "There's little worth remembering your whole life long, but once in a while some-one gets a few words right."

I waited to hear who had got a few words right. I thought of George Eliot's candle flickering, like the little ego of each of us that wants to be—demands to be—the centre of things. She had got that right. But I knew he wasn't talking about George Eliot. And for once he wasn't talking about himself.

"Yes. Marianne Rasmussen." He shook his head. He didn't say the lines out loud and I didn't press him. I could have named any number of lines or whole poems that qualified, yet there was one bit that floated into my mind and stayed there while we sat quietly under the small, high window, one each side of the book-laden table, in a truce of sorts. It wasn't anything profound; it did not get me out of myself and into sympathy with others; it was personal, I suppose, which is surprising since I couldn't remember it exactly, hadn't ever memorized it, so I couldn't be sure I had the words right. But its meaning—I got that. *And I am strangled, my own hands at my open throat.* It sounds as if it would belong to the Flesh Poems, but it was written before them, before whatever happened that changed her and her poetry. It made me remember my dream about the gravestone with my name on it. Was I strangling myself by being here in this house belonging to these men? One thing was sure: I wasn't getting any writing done. I wasn't writing any masterpieces down in that garden.

Aubrey broke into my thoughts. "Blake went further, you know, than Eliot. And I quote: '. . . every thing that lives, / Lives not alone, nor for itself.'"

"Oh," I said. "It's lovely. In its simplicity."

He got impatient. The hand waved between us as if of its own accord. He looked up to the skylights for help. The day was dull; only a foggy, impenetrable sky sat over us like a piece of felt. "You think he's talking about love. Don't you? He's talking about worms. You don't live for yourself alone because—if you're good for nothing else, at least you'll feed the worms."

For some minutes neither of us spoke. I thought about X wishing I were dead. But that was a dream, I reminded myself.

"Look," he said finally, "I'm sure you consider my views on marriage and family in general jaundiced. What others call love I see as a debilitating illness; it never worked any magic for me. Women. I couldn't put up with the whing-ing, the clinging, the endless desire to be close. The desire to interrupt my work." He had spoken directly to me but now retreated, and his next words, although they were matter-of-fact enough, seemed to come from his far shore. "Marianne was different, she was like me. God, she could be cold. Ruthless."

He stopped. He hadn't meant to speak out loud. He looked as if he'd been smacked. Seeing his mouth tremble, *I* felt cold. It was like love being taken away. I stopped breath-ing. It was like being betrayed all over again.

He didn't go on. He didn't tell me whatever he was remembering. After a few moments he said, "Her husband stuck with her, I heard, while I got my just rewards. Just this. Dying alone at the top of a house belonging to a brother who wishes I were somewhere else. Eh, Harry?"

110

"Harry isn't here," I said quietly.

He turned his gaze on me, not as if he were surprised to see me or didn't know who I was, but as if he saw, once again, what an inevitable small pimple I was in his life. "Ah well, you'll tell him. You tell him everything, don't you? If I ever say anything of the least interest."

"I think, Marianne—wasn't it in the service of her art? That she was like that? I mean, in order to write such fierce things." Words like axes, I was thinking, how they flash, and did that mean they wouldn't last? But if they hack at the ice within us... "Kafka," I said. "Words to pierce what's frozen in us."

He shook his head, not to deny what I'd said, or so I thought, but to clear his mind. He must have cleared it well; he fell silent. I looked up to the skylights. The day was still dull, the sky still impenetrable.

His voice, when he went on, was harsh. "'Did you come from a happy home?' some woman asked me, years ago. 'I did not come from a home,' I told her. 'I came from a house with two parents, and as soon as I had left the house, they refilled it with a brother.' Nineteen years between us. They couldn't live without me and made a substitute. Did you hear that, Harry?"

"Were you jealous?" I asked.

"I was gone," he said. "I've never had a home. Never owned a house, didn't want to. I never stopped long enough to belong to anyone or anywhere." I let him think about that, let him take some time to gaze around the beautiful space we sat in and lift his eyes to the windows and sky. "That is, until I came here, and you are right to wear that look on your knowing puss. I've been here... long." He sat up and pointed his finger at me. "It's because I kept myself apart that I could write. Loneliness aids vision. Don't you know that? I can see the moon through any of these windows, wherever it floats in the sky. I see it when it's full, when it's gibbous, when it's a sliver of itself. Who sees any farther than that?" He looked right at me. "Remember being a kid? Running outside, fast as you could, going nowhere, having nowhere in mind. Running in circles. Running down a road, going nowhere. I think of that, sitting here. Running just for the hell of it."

———————

I left the aerie quietly that day, in a kind of hush, feeling that I'd altered to accommodate what had happened between us. But in what way? I don't know; I can only say I felt a shift, and not just in sympathy for him. It seemed a good thing, but it was followed immediately by a return of the disquieting atmosphere that had surrounded me when I'd first arrived at the brothers' house. It was the same sense of impending grief, the feeling of coming precipitously to the end of things. Maybe it was only the effect of the shadowy light in the stairwell. It was, as I said before, a cloudy day.

———————

I seldom compared Harry to Aubrey anymore; they seemed dissimilar to me now that I knew them better. But one day when we were reading together in the garden, I looked up to see Harry plucking thoughtfully at his beard, and it was also a habit of Aubrey's, although in him, as with most of his gestures, it looked more theatrical than ruminative. Harry's beard was full and kept trimmed; Aubrey's was patchy and unkempt enough to have made me envision crumbs if not spiders and other creatures hiding in it. I said, "You must have been quite a surprise to your mother, arriving after nineteen years."

I suppose I startled Harry; his hand moved up to his forehead. When he did that, it was almost as if I saw his mother (and I'd never seen a photo of her) in his face. I felt he was unconsciously mirroring her. I wondered if I ever did that, channelling mine—an inconvenient thought because I then had to remember he was still calling me by my mother's name. He went on telling me about his mother, and I sat there thinking about mine, which led me to wondering how cold a person I was and if I was capable of loving anyone as I'd once believed I was.

I thought of Aubrey sitting alone upstairs under the little window that overlooked the garden. I glanced up and saw the blank pane reflecting very little light. "Harry," I said, "you designed such a beautiful room upstairs; it's really incredible, an almost spiritual space. Why did you give it to Aubrey?"

He shrugged. We listened to the birds rustle through the undergrowth for a minute. I figured that was the end of the conversation, but then Harry said, "I gave it to him because I hate him."

Even I knew better than to make any comment on that; nothing I could say would be right. He sighed and stretched out his legs, and I reached over and set my hand as lightly as I could on his knee.

"And because my mother asked me not to hate him," he added. He picked up my hand and held it in both of his, and then he raised it to his lips and kissed it.

I told him, "You've made me think of my mother."

"What was she like?"

"Harry, I've given you her name. I mean, you asked me my name, when I came here, and I didn't give it to you. I gave

you her name instead. I was afraid—I was afraid you'd recognize my name, because I've done some writing, published
a book and some magazine and newspaper articles that you
or Aubrey might have heard of." My voice had wound down
by the time I'd finished saying that. The explanation was so
ludicrous. Even other writers didn't know who I was. I was
the kind of writer who is asked by polite strangers, "Oh? Will
I have heard of you?" My face blazed with the shame of it. "It
was crazy of me. Honestly, I don't know what I was thinking."
    "Instinct," Harry said. "You instinctively lied."
    "But I don't. I'm not a liar, really I'm not."
    "Well, you are a writer," he said, with a little smile. "So I
assume you have your own kind of truth. Are you going to
tell me now? Who you are?"
    "I'm so ashamed."
    "Me too. I don't really hate him, you know."
    "I know. I can tell."
    "He wasn't always like this. Not as bad as this. Age is a bug-
ger. Pulls out the stops, in a whole different way."
    "Yeah."
    "And so?"
    And so I told him my real name. He didn't pretend he'd
heard of me; he said he liked my name and could he call me
by it now and I said yes. He stroked my cheek and my hair,
and then he leaned forward and kissed me a long and very
gentle kiss. It was a somewhat chaste kiss actually, and it
bruised my ego—truth be told. Just before it ended I added a
little pressure, a little buzz of my own. He seemed surprised
but not displeased.

———————

The next day, when we were strolling home with our groceries, Harry said, "You've gone to a lot of trouble to write this book of yours, but I don't understand why the subterfuge. Aubrey was always going to like the idea of a biography. Some writers wouldn't, but he, at this stage, couldn't resist. A legacy. It's what he's always wanted."

We were on a whole new footing, Harry and I, and I wanted to tell him the truth, I really did, but how could I blurt it out on the street? I danced around it. "Writers are wary of biographers. They want the legacy, for sure, but not at the cost of letting people learn some of the less savoury facts about them. And then there's always conjecture. Biographers are famous for inventing a slant, for guessing at motives and repercussions. You know, how it must have *felt*."

I'd been almost flippant in my desire to avoid having to tell the truth, but something in my own words reminded me of a story I'd written about a biographer. I hadn't thought of it for ages. As we lugged our groceries, in our ecologically helpful bags, towards the house on Ontario Street, I tried to recall the details, although I didn't know if I'd had anything illuminating to say on the subject. It was one of my failures.

I found the story on my laptop and asked Harry if he would read it for me. He must have thought it an odd request, but he didn't say so. I didn't understand it myself.

## The Art of Biography

Our biographer seemed young to us, and vulnerable, but we could not always be as kind to him as he wanted us to be. We had our lives to live and he—well, he was more often than not in the way, trying to see over our shoulders (seeing what you see, he called it, which shows how clueless he could be) and stopping us in the midst of whatever we were doing and asking us to explain ourselves. Pointing out when we were contradictory too. "Five minutes ago you said you longed for peace, A." That kind of thing. And then I might snap at him, "Because you had your nose in my armpit," or some such thing. If it was on the crude side, so much the better for shutting him up and setting him back on his heels. And if I ever answered a question with "Who wants to know?" he would fade, visibly fade into a pale version of himself, and shrink too, before my eyes. I would be forced to look away, to seek some inanimate object, let's say a desk; it might well be a desk. I would stare at the thing until he left the room. He would never leave the house, not unless we went out, and when we went in different directions, I one way and B the other, oh what a quandary for the poor fellow. I don't know how he decided which to follow, and the worst part of it was he knew he couldn't dither, because to dither could be to lose us both. Once in a while exactly that happened, and whichever of us returned home first would find him on the doorstep in a pitiable pose, a heap of indecision and dejection. The long lines either side of his nose and mouth that so defined him were etched, I believe, as he sat on that doorstep.

Why did he need to study us? We certainly didn't invite him to write our lives, and I don't think he found us all that fascinating. B said he'd tire of us, but over the years he remained as dedicated as ever. I had first noticed him, or so I recalled, in the schoolyard when I was six. Oh yes, we have known him almost forever. The day I remember catching sight of him was also the day I first met B, so without really thinking about it, I assumed he was connected in some way, either to B or to our meeting. B said he'd turned up the day of his grandmother's death, at the moment B bent to kiss his dead grandmother's cold face. When I learned that, I remembered that someone had followed me the day I tried to run away from my family, and the more I thought about it the surer I became that he was the one who'd followed me. I was four at the time, the same age B was when his grandmother died. All of this synchronicity made us think our falling in love and marrying must have been preordained, or why would our biographer have shown such an interest in the two of us before we'd even met? We did occasionally wonder if it was possible he could wish to write the biographies of others as well as ours, but we considered this impractical; he really spent all his time with us.

There are times when a couple needs privacy. I asked him outright before we were married if he planned to spy on us, if he had cut holes into the eyes of the daisies on our bedroom wallpaper, that sort of thing. What a pained expression answered that. I was only teasing him; he was quite a prude, and I don't expect he would have wanted to see us naked, much less to peep at our lovemaking. Nor do I think he had much imagination where our bodies were concerned. References to body parts and functions nearly turned him inside out.

We sometimes tried to get rid of him. Once, frustrated beyond endurance, we drove him out into the country and abandoned him. Once we took him with us to the city and hid in the changing rooms in a large department store. We employed a number of ruses to lose him, but he always turned up on our doorstep, and although we didn't know why it was, neither of us had the heart to refuse to let him in.

I can recall a time when we felt flattered by his attention, possibly because in those earlier days he was obviously critical of us in general and cynical about our abilities as well as our intentions. I used to hate to think what he wrote about us when he sat down to his computer at the end of each day.

We thought we'd die before he did, that being the natural order of things between subjects and their biographer. We noticed that he was failing, but we were aging too. When it became apparent that his health was seriously compromised, we started slowing down, taking more rest than we needed so he would too, and getting him to visit our doctor when we had appointments. But he, although weakened, remained indefatigable, and if anything increased his surveillance of us. We thought it possible he hardly slept.

I have not mentioned our most compelling years: our youth, our courtship, the challenges of marriage and children, the ups and downs of family life and careers, all of which he faithfully recorded. But now that I am writing about him, rather than vice versa, those times and events blur in my mind, and he—whose life seemed so uneventful, so bland and timid and soft and pale—he waits on the doorstep of my memory as the greatest tragedy I have ever known. B feels the same. If we had known what was going to happen, we'd have arranged a double suicide before he passed away. Honestly, I think we'd have died happy. Our lives are nothing to us now.

Here is the response from the one literary magazine I sent the story to:

Dear _____

Thank you for sending us your submission. Our reviewers found it had merit, but decided it was not quite suitable for publication in our Review. The following comments were recorded by one of our readers: "Replace the premise of dissatisfaction with one of desire. Who wants what? A fine effort. Keep writing."

Please feel free to try us again during our reading period, September 30th to June 1st.

Sincerely,

_____

for:

_____,

Fiction Editor

I thought perhaps the one reader who commented was right about the story. "Who wants what?" The basis of every plot in the world. I thought maybe wanting was the only thing to write about. But didn't the biographer in the story want something? Surely anyone who exhibited such tenacity must want something. But for the life of me, I didn't know what it was.

Over the laptop at the kitchen table, Harry said, "Is it the joint consciousness of the couple that has created the biographer?"

I said, "What?"

"Clearly he isn't real. So isn't he something they created, together? And whatever they think about him, whether it's positive or negative, that's what he is. At any given time. He's their memories, isn't he? That they can't get rid of."

"Oh," I said.

"There isn't any context given for their lives," Harry noted. "Obviously, they've been together for many years, since they were kids. So they created this thing you call the biographer, the equivalent of a god or a judge of them, not of them individually, but of them together. And after he left them, they thought it would have been better for them to have died before he did, because now no one will remember them. Or worse, they won't remember themselves, the way they were. The thing they had between them is gone, and so—"

"Their lives are over." I was awed. "You mean this is about a failed marriage, don't you?" I had not seen the story in that way at all; I'd taken my own story completely literally. I'd thought it was about the biographer. "Does the biographer want something?" I asked.

"I don't know," Harry said. "It's confused. What do people want?"

"I guess... to have a meaningful life."

"And what makes life meaningful?" he asked.

You do, Harry, I thought. Involuntarily. Completely involuntarily. Out of left field, that thought. And immediately I was stricken. What if I meant it?

"How do you know all this?" I asked.

He smiled and said, "Shucks." But then, seriously, he said, "I know all this because I was in a relationship for several years, and your story made me think of it, of her and our time together. And the way it ended. Just like in the story, what we had together died. If you think about it that way, you won't be so afraid."

I looked into his face and remembered I was still lying to him. "There's something you should know," I said. No way to be delicate about it, so I blurted it out. "I'm not writing about Aubrey. I'm writing about Marianne Rasmussen."

Harry took hold of my hands. "It's okay," he said. "Don't worry. I figured that's what you were up to."

"I don't even know why. My friends say I'm obsessed. I am obsessed."

"Hey. It doesn't matter why. It's something you need to do. That's enough."

———————

We took our meal in the garden, sitting at the small table, nearly touching. The evening was one of those still, velvety, going-on-forever Toronto evenings. You think they'll never end, but of course like everything they end, and afterwards he walked me to my makeshift bedroom. We chatted as we passed through the kitchen and went down the hall. We kept our voices low, which made it feel as if we were playing a game for two. At my door he stood over me, listening to me while I finished a bit of nonsense, that look of tender amusement on his face, that Cary Grant kind of good manners. He caught me off guard when he swept me into his arms and kissed me. A full body kiss this time, with an erection I couldn't ignore pressing into me. My body didn't ignore it—my body responded, but my mind went the other way and I stepped back.

"Hey," Harry said. "I didn't mean to frighten you."

The caress was back in his voice when he said goodnight. That was the part of the exchange that frightened me.

# { 11 }

I WALKED UP to the aerie with a spring in my step thinking I should have got myself a Nike T-shirt like the Necropolis woman wore. I had seen the real Nike, the goddess of victory, at the Louvre, standing at the top of a flight of marble stairs with her marble wings outspread, sturdy as Kate Winslet at the prow of the Titanic and without a man behind her. Victory spelled with a capital V. But headless. There is always a cost. I discounted the cost as I climbed the stairs. I would have liked to see Aubrey's expression if I'd had one of those T-shirts to wear, but it didn't dampen my enthusiasm to stride in without it.

He smiled when he saw me, went on smiling as he watched me cross the room. I didn't sit down when I reached him; I stood over him. "Hey," I said jauntily.

"Hey," he said, as if friendly.

When he wanted to draw you to him, he always could. So I wavered. Even standing over him, looking down on him, I wavered, and instead of asking outright for Marianne Rasmussen's papers as I'd intended, I said, "I know you have quite a collection of papers, Aubrey, notes and drafts of your work and so on."

"Letters and such from other writers," he said, adding the logical end of my sentence.

"All kinds of things," I said. I couldn't believe the sound that came out of me. The voice. Chirp, chirp, head to the side, apologetic giggle barely repressed.

He spoke before I could. "Good thing I have a fireplace." He pointed it out in case I hadn't noticed the great gaping maw in the wall. "One of these days," he told me gently, "I'll have a fire."

---

My attempt at assertion had ended in mortification, and it took a full day to recover, a day I stayed away from Aubrey Ash in order to revive some semblance of self. I asked Harry if he knew why Aubrey taunted me, why he was so keen for me to know that at any moment, left on his own as he often was, he might destroy the documents I wanted just so he could tell me gleefully that he'd done it. But what difference did it make why the man wanted to rile me? My real anxiety was that he would do it.

Harry listened, as he did whenever I spoke. Side by side, we lounged on my couch (it was a rainy day, no garden tryst for us), and I tried to explain what he already understood, or seemed to understand: my love for Rasmussen's poetry, my quest to find out all I could about her work. "I don't want her lost," I said. "I'm afraid she could be, all those incredible poems could be lost. Gone. As if they'd never been written. That's what happens without critical response, without some kind of boosting. And a woman. From the West. Already marginalized, a double disadvantage. People need to know." Harry didn't remonstrate that I might not be the only one who could save Marianne Rasmussen. He didn't laugh at me for thinking that I was.

Rain fell and fell outside our windows, patient and insistent, as if the sky were saying, It's my funeral and I'll cry if I want to.

"I know Aubrey has letters of hers," I said. "Drafts of poems maybe."

"And you want to see them."

"God, yes. I need to read them, copy them, get them into an archive."

"Ah" was all he said.

"Do you know where they are? Where he keeps them?"

He groaned and shifted his arm, which had been around my shoulders. "I can guess where they are," he said cautiously. "You'll have to ask him for them."

"I've hinted I want to read them. I haven't come right out and asked for them. He's so forbidding sometimes. And photos, he has photos too."

"I don't know that he has any you would use."

"Well, I can't know when I haven't seen them."

"Right."

"And photos, of the kind that are unusual, not the run of the mill that anyone can dredge up from her acquaintances, would help the publication of the book."

"Right," he said again.

He disapproved, I knew he did, but I pushed on. "I'm afraid he'll destroy the stuff he has. To spite me, to spite everyone. I think... maybe you could help me? These documents are valuable; they belong to the future. Couldn't we get them away? I don't mean give them to me, but put them somewhere safe?"

"I don't think we can do that," Harry said.

That night I had an awful nightmare. In the eerily concrete way of dreams, it was born with a specific setting and a named main character. A little boy. In the dream I knew his name. I was a boy too. We were about seven years old and we were being kept in a dark basement. In the darkness the other boy was lighting matches at a gas flame, his eyes alight too when each match burst into flames. It was forbidden to do that. I told on him. A man descended and lit the boy's hand on fire. Put it in water, I thought, but there was none. He flapped it, all aflame, his eyes on me, surprise in them at the pain and his new fate.

———————

Aubrey sent word the next morning that he wasn't well enough for our interview.

"What's wrong?" I asked.

"No reason to panic," Harry said. I must have looked alarmed. I felt alarmed; my nightmare came back to me. Harry said, "He didn't sleep well and he's tired. That's all."

I went out for groceries on my own because Harry said he had things to do. I worried about that; usually he was happy to go with me. I wondered if my revelations of the night before had disappointed him enough that he didn't want to spend time with me. I tried to rush through the shopping, then got in line behind a crazy person who demanded to see the manager over the price of toilet paper, and an old man who had to count out every penny. He held me up even after his bill was paid. He walked away from the cash register and left his cane leaning against the counter and I had to call him back. I handed it to him and he didn't even grunt, didn't even look up to see who'd helped him, much less thank me. "Nice of him to share his sunshine," I said to the clerk. She glanced up from the groceries, surprised.

By the time I finally headed back to the house, I was imagining the worst: I'd alarmed Harry enough he'd decided he needed to warn Aubrey to watch out for me. He'd told Aubrey I might try to get the loot out from under him. "Blood is thicker than water," I muttered. No one on the sidewalk paid any attention to me; most of them were talking too, either into their phones or to themselves; it's a solipsistic world.

A plane flew through the sky, a tiny thing, way up high in the clouds over the treetops and the tallest buildings. Could I really believe there were tiny people inside it? Real people? No, I could not. And if they were real, and could look down and see me, smaller than an ant, not one of them would know or care that I had a book to write.

---

The police arrived at the house on Ontario Street, sirens screeching, at the same time I turned the corner. I thought it must be a fire, that the house had caught fire while I was gone. But there were no fire trucks. Three cop cars pulled up, red lights flashing, to block the street, and then one drove ahead as an ambulance arrived. I set my bags down on the pavement. Everything happened quickly and more like a movie unspooling than an incident on the street where I lived. Officers bolted from their vehicles and ran to the brothers' house. But to which side? I picked up my bags and inched closer.

Before I could get near enough to see the front of the house, I was stopped. "Stay back, ma'am," a young female officer told me, her arm raised, militaristic palm towards me. I stayed back. One of the officers who had run from his car came down the path from the house, helping a hobbling man. There was blood on the front of his T-shirt. After him came another officer, with another person who could barely walk. I had just thought of blood being thicker than water and now I realized how seldom you see real blood, a lot of blood, see it soaked into someone's shirt like a rose, a big summer rose darkened by sun, see it splashed onto someone's legs. These were not the Ash brothers, but even as I ascertained that they were not, that they were some raggedly dressed down-and-outers unknown to me, I felt sick with fear. A woman, with the skeletal look of those who don't know how to stop what they should never have started, tottered down the path next, fighting with the officer who held her arm, swearing at everyone, including me when she spotted me staring. She was holding onto her other arm, and it was covered in blood; from the shoulder to the wrist, her shirtsleeve was a dark, wet red. Her splayed fingers dug into the elbow, propping it up, holding it on.

Efficiently, all three of the victims were put into the ambulance and it screamed away. Then two of the officers went up the path to the Ash brothers' door. "That's my house," I told the female officer, picking up my bags.

"Just hold on," she said. "I'll tell you when you can go."

So I had to wait on the sidewalk, trembling in case whatever had happened to the victims I'd seen had happened to Harry and Aubrey. My legs were too weak to hold me. I sat down on the curb. In some of the windows opposite, neighbours were watching. Two of the police cars drove

128

off. One neighbour fellow came out to talk to me, but the policewoman shooed him off. I asked her what she knew of the situation and she said she knew nothing; they'd had a call about an altercation in the house, that was all. "In the evil twin," I said, and she stared down at me. "The house next door, it's falling down." She nodded in matter-of-fact agreement.

It bothered me that I had thought of blood on a man's shirt as a rose, almost dry at the edges of the petals and blasted at the centre. I thought it wasn't the right way to think about blood, about hurt. What if it was Harry? I couldn't let myself think of him like that. I tried to see him as I'd last seen him in the kitchen when he told me he didn't have time to get the groceries with me. There had been something wrong between us. He was disappointed in me. I hadn't realized it would bother me so much.

And then the waiting was over. "All clear," the woman cop said. Doors slammed, the police drove away, and I was allowed to return. I avoided stepping on the blood spatters on the sidewalk, some of which still looked wet. I let myself into the quiet house, stopping at the staircase, looking up. Not a sound. They would have heard me come in, but Harry didn't come down or call. I set my bags down once again and started up the stairs. When I reached the second floor landing, I stopped long enough to call to Harry in a voice that sounded tremulous in my own ears.

"Up here," he hollered, quite cheerfully I thought.

He was sitting with Aubrey. They hailed me with wide smiles; they knew more than I did about the goings-on, and were pleased to have an audience. Harry had made the call to the police, having heard the disturbance next door. He said it had sounded as if there were a crowd of them and every one of them was bouncing off the walls. He'd called the police while he stood outside the front door, listening to the curses and screams. He hadn't attempted to intervene, "Not being stupid," Aubrey said. He appeared shaken, and was looking at Harry with the only ounce of approbation I'd ever seen him exhibit towards his brother.

"There were just the three of them, making enough noise for an army," Harry said.

I said I'd seen them brought out, and there had been considerable bleeding.

"They'd been sleeping there, but not for long I expect, after a night as high as kites."

"So they were fighting amongst themselves? There wasn't someone attacking them?"

"With friends like those..." Harry said. "Incidents like this bring out the clichés," he added with a shrug.

I went down to the kitchen and unloaded the groceries. Some frozen peas were now thawed and I debated refreezing them, then decided to make soup from them. Tossing the bag into the refrigerator, I recalled that in a first aid course I'd been told a bag of frozen peas could make a decent cold pack, and I wondered if I would have been clear-headed enough to pull it out of my bag and apply it to the wounds of the worst of the victims if I'd arrived on the scene a few minutes earlier than I did. Would I have rushed to help them, not knowing who was victim and who perpetrator? Not knowing which one of them had wielded the knife and maybe still had it and might stab me?

I served the fresh pea soup cold for lunch with a dollop of sour cream and chives. I took it upstairs and the three of us ate together. The brothers made a fuss about how wonderful the soup was, and I admitted to loving food, which meant I loved to make it. That was an innocent comment. I hadn't intended to refer to anything to do with art, nothing but cooking was on my mind, but Aubrey, in charitable mode again, made the link. "You have put your finger on it," he said. "Love is at the heart of making any form of art."

And not intellectual love, I thought. He might have remembered our conversation about Murdoch and Eliot and Rasmussen, but I didn't think so; it seemed he existed in self-contained episodes, and I reflected that I was doing the same lately. It wasn't a thought I wanted to pursue. We sat for a few minutes in unusual amity, with them gazing inwards too, I supposed, and then Harry pointed out that Aubrey had slumped down in his chair. He'd fallen asleep. "Too much excitement," Harry said.

---

The next morning while Harry and I were sipping our second cups of coffee and sharing sections of the newspaper, we were interrupted by a sharp knocking at the door. "That'll be police," Harry said, and went to answer.

The front hall being some distance from the table at the back of the kitchen, I could hear only the faint timbre of two male voices. I returned to my paper, but the ever diversionary American politics didn't hold my attention. I began to think maybe it wasn't the police at the door, keeping Harry talking so long; I began to think I knew who it was. It was my husband. It was X. He had come to tell me he was worried about me, that I didn't belong here and he was going to take me away. I imagined Harry coming back to the kitchen looking different than I had seen him look before, looking upset, saying, It's for you.

I would go to the door. It would be X standing there in the foyer under the fancy old light fixture, on the house side of the old oak door, solid as a person could be, lines etched in his face that I hadn't seen before. I'd slip behind him, not say a word, usher him out of the house, close the door, give him a what-the-fuck stare.

I've been worried about you, he would say. I would look up to the elms. It was a muggy day and they wouldn't signal anything; they wouldn't move so much as a twig or leaf. You don't belong here, he would say. He would point out the blood spatters on the sidewalk, the yellow caution tape that swagged the evil twin. I'm going to take you home, he would say, standing an inch away from me, making me feel like the leaves overhead flopped on the heavy air. *Forgiveness like the soft underarm of the over forties.*

"Was it the police?" I asked when Harry came back. Yes, he said, it was the police.

———————————

The feeling I'd had before, the sense of coming to the end of things, came down strong on me that day. I kept picturing Aubrey asleep in his chair, the way we'd left him the night before. It had been a shock, seeing him huddled there, his breathing so shallow we'd had to watch for a minute to be sure he hadn't died. If only he had, I could not help thinking, if only we were at the end of all this.

I didn't belong here. In this house belonging to men. I didn't know what I was doing here, contemplating stealing what didn't belong to me. But stealing those papers was on my mind. I needed them, and Aubrey was never voluntarily going to give them to me.

132

And why did Aubrey Ash have Marianne Rasmussen's papers anyway? Why should they belong to him? There he was, nestled in his aerie, an old man holding onto a woman's papers. Doing nothing with them, consigning them to dust, willing them to disintegrate along with his own. How could I risk leaving her legacy to the whim of an old man?

———————

I didn't believe for a minute that Aubrey had stored Marianne's papers in the basement; old drafts of his stories maybe, letters from lesser-known writers sure, but not the valuable papers. They would be in his room, not far from the fireplace that was kept laid and ready to light. I pictured the sparsely furnished apartment above me. There were only a few places he could have hidden the things I wanted, and he slept so soundly I thought I should be able to find them without waking him. I only had to wait in my makeshift room until night fell right down into darkness and silence and I could be sure the brothers were asleep.

Since Aubrey might keep the various materials loose in a drawer and they might be too slippery to carry down the stairs without dropping, I tucked two soft, folded grocery bags under my arm. I intended to bring the letters and whatever else I found downstairs with me. I would stay up all night perusing them, and then I would take them back and replace them where I'd found them. And of course before returning them I would, with my phone, photograph them. I already saw myself snapping away. Whatever else happened, I would save copies of these artifacts for the future.

I didn't pretend I wasn't betraying the man's trust. And I didn't believe I could be exonerated just because some future literary historians would thank me. No, it was with full knowledge of my duplicity, and black of heart but determined, that I forged ahead.

---

What a piece of work is a man, and a man of a hundred, sleeping on his back in a moonlit room, appears at first glance to be all nose. The flesh falls away and all that remains is a thin scrape of cartilage jutting out. The sight didn't give me pause, but it did make me feel the blood pulsing in my younger veins.

There was no desk in the room. I had, from the first time I walked into the space, searched for the likeliest hiding places for his cache. I quaked at the likeliest one of all, his bedside stand, which had three drawers. I thought I'd better look through the cupboards either side of the kitchenette sink, and the bathroom cabinets too, before I tackled the stand so close to Aubrey, who was gasping, crumpled mouth gaping, only a few times a minute. I went to the bathroom first, gliding in between shadows, feeling like a phantom in someone else's dream.

The narrow upper shelves of the bathroom cabinet held nothing but the old man's shaving and toothbrushing equipment and the medications he'd stopped taking, all past the expiry date. Below the sink were the usual toilet paper, wipes, cleaning supplies, rags, and a stained sitz bath that made me shudder. The cupboards in the main room held nothing for me. The bedside stand was all that was left, unless he stored things under his bed.

Creeping near, I bent and picked up a corner of the sheet. Nothing but dust fluffs the size of crocodiles.

With my hand on the knob of the top drawer, I gazed down on Aubrey Ash, who lay with his pitiful snake-veined hands crossed over his chest. He'd gone to sleep prepared to die and hadn't managed it. I tried to breathe in his rhythm. I could not do it; the man was barely clinging to existence. It had to be a very deep sleep. Good. I slid the drawer open. And there they were. What else did he need beside him at night? A glass of water on the bedside stand, and inside, the remains of his life. I reached out my index finger, already rehearsing how I would flick through the stacked envelopes as I looked for return addresses. Aubrey snorted. I froze. It was seconds before I turned and saw that his eyes were open. He was not wearing his sunglasses; his eyes were looking for the first time directly into mine.

# { 12 }

HE SPOKE, his voice gravelly and so quiet I had to hold my breath to hear him, and what he said was, "My mind and my spirit have their own liberty." His eyes were blue, the irises heavily clouded at the rims. He could not look piercingly at me, although I was sure he tried.

"Saul Bellow," I said, leaning right over him and staring back.

Calmly, he said, "Fuck you."

I said, "I want them. As your biographer, I need them."

"They belong to me."

"But Aubrey, you can't take them with you. Give them to the world."

He tried to raise his head off the pillow and immediately sank back. He said, "Do you think for one fucking minute I believed you? I know whose letters you want. Whose photos you want. Whose biography you're writing."

"Okay, and what do you want?" I let my gaze drift again to the open drawer where my fingers lay inches from the prize.

"You and your literary biography." He was breathing unevenly, gasping between words. "It's laughable. Earnestly pursuing your quest. As if you're the one who's going to tell the world how to write a masterpiece. It's not the world who wants to know anyway. It's you, you poor—deluded fool."

"Calm down," I said. "Breathe." It's the kind of thing men like to say to women, and it had the same effect. It made him mad as hell.

He hauled himself up on his elbows. "You think she'd help you, teach you how. Her magic would rub off on you. Her letters would tell you how to write her poems. Well, here's the rub, madam. Maybe they would, maybe they would. But you wouldn't know how to use it. Don't you see? Knowing it—if there's some one thing to know—is only part of the equation. What good is a key if you have nothing locked inside? Hmm? Look at me." He pounded his bony chest. I looked away. "Nothing in there to open. Nothing to say. Nothing needing to be said. I said—look at me."

"Is that it? Is that what you want? For people to look at you?" I suppose I said it with more than a little disdain. I felt affronted in some moral way, as if he were the one who'd been caught red-handed.

He grabbed hold of my arm. His grip wasn't strong, but it held me there.

I said, "Next you'll be telling me I need to penetrate further. To see you. So fucking male. I don't see you? You don't see anything. That's why you can't think for yourself. That's why you quote Saul Bellow instead of thinking up something original to say. Something of your own."

Neither of us had noticed Harry standing at the top of the stairs. We thought we were alone until he asked what was going on. Aubrey's breath, breaking in harsh croaks, became the only sound after that. Harry strode over to the bed and looked down on him.

"My sunglasses," Aubrey said. He let go of my arm and clutched at his crenelated old sternum.

"Lie back," Harry told him. He found the glasses where Aubrey had left them on the bed beside him, and slid them onto his face. Aubrey sank back onto his pillow. He crossed his hands over his chest in his deathbed position. His breathing continued ragged; his lips were turning blue.

"Are you having a heart attack?" Harry asked him.

I said, "Maybe he should sit up, actually."

A couple of squawks came out of him before he could speak and then he said, "Fuck no, I'm not having a heart attack. I wouldn't give her the satisfaction."

Harry reached between me and the bed and slammed the drawer closed. "Go to bed," he told me. "I'll sit up with him until he stabilizes."

"Stabilizes," Aubrey said. "What a fucking choice of word. Wait. Tell her to wait."

I had started towards the stairs and turned to hear what he had to say. I could hardly see him since he was lying flat on the bed. But in the dark room, lit by the moon, Harry stood out like a disillusioned ghost. He was wearing a white T-shirt and blue striped pyjama bottoms, and his white hair stuck out every which way.

"I have a bit of information for you," Aubrey said. His voice was so weak and raspy I had to move closer to hear him. "Marianne isn't dead."

Right away I figured he was lying. Wasn't he? He had to be. But what an incredible lie. And for what? I watched Harry for a clue, but Harry, if he had any idea what Aubrey was up to, didn't show any reaction at all. He looked tired, tired and deeply discouraged.

"In fact, you've seen her," Aubrey cackled. He managed to raise his head, I suppose to see me, or more likely to direct his information at me since he likely could not see anything with his Ray-Bans on in the dark room.

I had to play my part, so I asked him what he meant.

"She spoke to you. You could have spoken to her. But you didn't avail yourself of the opportunity. No, you hurried away, you turned your back on her, you spurned her."

I said, "I really have no idea what you're talking about."

"No, you wouldn't. All your talk about seeing. As if you know how to see. You're *blind*. You've failed to see what's in front of your eyes."

For a mad moment I thought he meant he was Marianne Rasmussen, not physically, but that he'd written her poems. I thought he was going to make that monstrous, infamous claim, and the thought of it brought me right up to the bed in a manner that might have looked aggressive.

Harry stepped in front of me.

"I'm not going to hurt him," I said, annoyed. "I simply want to hear exactly what it is he's saying. The old charlatan."

"Name calling?" Aubrey said. "Your true nature is bursting forth, dear lady." He lay back again, panting.

"Just spit it out," I said. "Marianne Rasmussen is alive and I've seen her. Go on. Please. Continue."

"What do you think happens to poets when they get old, eh?" His voice quavered, but he pushed on, talking in spurts, breathing in between. "Ask yourself—if Marianne ever once made—as much money on her little chapbooks as—you've made writing about her—in journals and anthologies. Talking about her at conferences." His voice had got stronger as he went on, and more and more sarcastic, yet I felt I knew him better now. He was letting himself be known, and I understood his anger and frustration, I even shared it until he said, "You saw her in the corner store, down at Queen and Ontario, woman! You saw her, you heard her. For Christ's sake, you smelled her."

"No," I said.

"And you walked away. Didn't you? You couldn't walk away fast enough."

I sat down on the bed; it was a king-sized bed and I sat at the opposite corner from Aubrey. I couldn't have gone on standing. Could it be true? Could it be true? Marianne, that woman? Could I find her? They would know her, the people at the corner store. They could tell me how to find her.

But there was more to this. What was the more? My mind spun like a stalled computer, its little circle whirling endlessly. Finally it came to the realization it had been seeking. "How do you know about that woman? How do you know I saw that woman?"

"Saw her, heard her curses, smelled her," he muttered.

Harry came and sat beside me. He tried to take my hand, but I wasn't having it. "I want an answer," I said, and I said it to both of them.

I got no answer; they looked away from me. They had never seemed more alike than in their refusal. "Our Mutual Friend," I said. "More mutual than I knew."

# { 13 }

AUBREY ASH DIED that night. Harry had fallen asleep in the chair beside his bed and woke early in the morning to find that his brother wasn't breathing and was already cold to the touch. Aubrey, when I saw him, lay in state on the bed, his hands crossed over his chest. I wondered if he had arranged the dramatic display himself, as he had rehearsed it in the days before his death, or if he'd been unable at the end to achieve it, and his brother had done it for him. One thing you know immediately when you see death: it is nothing like sleep. I asked if I could touch Aubrey, and Harry said I could, so I laid my fingers on the thin, shiny skin of one old hand. The flesh underneath had turned a dusky blue. It was almost beautiful. I remembered that hand grasping at the air, trying to grab hold of something, anything, and Aubrey being annoyed at the sight of it and its instinctual greed. I remembered it grabbing my arm. It felt like plastic now, cool and solid and incapable of moving. Good, I thought, the fight is over. You didn't lose. And I believed Marianne, present with us, thought the same. I felt her sigh and it seemed like acceptance. It almost seemed like peace.

As I walked away from the bed, just as I reached the stairwell, a dizzy sensation took hold of me, and I had to clutch the railing and wait a few seconds before I could descend. I would have sat down on the top step and put my head into my hands if Harry hadn't been watching. As it was I simply took myself carefully down the stairs.

---

Of course the woman in the corner store was not Marianne Rasmussen; I spent a sleepless night reassuring myself of that. I had visited Marianne's grave. I had stood on the spot while her husband was buried in the plot beside her, years after she was laid there. I had spoken to his cousin, who had been present at her sickbed and at her funeral and at her interment, a witness to each step from hospital to burial. There was never the slightest reason to believe Aubrey was doing anything but baiting me and letting me know that he'd been in contact with Ryan Benson all along, that the two of them had corresponded before I ever came along, and continued to communicate during my tenure in the house. The idea of the poor old woman being Rasmussen wasn't all that farfetched, however, since Marianne's success was only literary. She had never made money from her extraordinary books. As Aubrey said, only the industry that grew up around her work made any money.

---

Harry confirmed I was right about Aubrey's deliberate mischief-making, or at least the part about the wild old woman, without my having to ask him. He confirmed that the incident had been related in a letter from Ryan Benson. He brought it up over coffee, after Aubrey's body had been removed from the house. He didn't volunteer any information about the matter that was uppermost in my mind that morning, although I'm sure he knew what it was and how anxious I was to have the issue resolved. I couldn't bring it up myself—it would have been too crass—but I had hoped he would help me out, let me know what might happen next, what I could expect. I was disappointed to get nothing from him—more than disappointed, I was frightened, worried, hurt—and it was only by reminding myself that I had disappointed him that I could find his silence at all acceptable. Believing he needed time to decide on his next steps, I said I would go out and get us something for lunch. He said he had an appointment at noon and would be gone for the afternoon, and I could suit myself about lunch. He was so solemn, I didn't ask if he had dinner plans too.

I did not go upstairs again after Aubrey's body left the house, although I pictured the bedside stand with its three drawers, and I could feel the handle of the top one in my hand. I could feel the drawer sliding out. I could see the envelopes stacked in there. Just thinking about it made the bottom fall out of my day. There had been a club; I hadn't known of its existence and had never been in line for membership. That undeniable fact numbed me. No, I didn't go upstairs again. Marianne's letters and photos and whatever else she left behind were inviolable now; I couldn't touch them without authorization, and that had never looked less likely.

———————

I opened the front door of the house and hesitated before crossing the threshold. I was not sure I could bridge the gap, or even put one foot in front of the other to walk. The outside world before me, trees, cars, other houses blurred. Above me the elms murmured in polite, insipid sympathy. They knew worse was to come.

---

I came to the derelict corner store at the intersection of Ontario and Queen, and was surprised to be there, having no recollection of walking those blocks. This time, entering the store, I wasn't assailed by the reek of urine, and no grey-haired, raging old woman cursed at me. The young man behind the counter, which was stacked with pineapples, on for $4.49, greeted me with a weary nod and went back to his sudoku. I bought a bottle of water and drank it while I waited for the streetcar.

The traffic whipped past; everyone wanted to leave the district as quickly as they could. A woman, on foot, rounded the far corner and came towards me. Something about her was familiar; I thought it was probably her gait. She was making a complicated job of walking, as many do who have ingested or imbibed too much of what may seem to be a good thing at the time. As she came closer I saw that her right arm was bandaged, and she was holding it as if it were in a sling, although I could see no sling. A ripple of fear went through me at the thought of her passing me, inches from me, as she was set to do. That was irrational; she was in her own world and looked unlikely to notice me or anyone else. She approached without a degree of focus in her eyes. I only had to step aside to let her pass; in seconds she'd be walking away. It was a miracle she could keep to the sidewalk, I thought, just as she didn't. She fell at my feet.

"Oh," I said, retreating a little as she stretched full out on her back on the pavement. She looked right at me and said "Oh" too, mocking me with the exact same tone of voice. I thought she was about my age and about my build as well, but way thinner, with a look of having been eroded from the inside.

"Can I help you? Do you want to get up?" I asked. She was giving no indication that she did want to get back on her feet.

She pointed her finger at me, waving it, and said, "I know you."

"Yes." It was inevitable, wasn't it?

"I saw you with your grocery bags."

"Yes."

"You remember me, right? I lived next door to you."

"Right," I said. "But not for long." It was more than a little odd to be looking down at her, the way she lay sprawled on the sidewalk at my feet. She reached up and took hold of my jeans just below the knee. Cars were slowing to gawk at us. An SUV pulled up to the curb and the driver, a man in his fifties, I guessed, asked if the woman was bothering me, if he should call the police. "Do you need help?" I asked the woman. "Can we give you a hand?" She said she had two of her own, ha ha. I shrugged and the fellow drove away.

I thought of asking her about the man who'd stayed in the house with her, the one whose blood looked like a rose, if he had survived, but I feared she might have been the one who knifed him. "The streetcar's coming," I told her. I could see it down a few blocks.

"Don't worry about it," she said.

"I'm taking it," I said. "Are you?"

She closed her eyes. I started to worry about leaving her there if she'd overdosed, but after a few seconds she opened her eyes, shook her head as if to say I was incorrigible, and

145

one-armed, hauled herself to a sitting position. Shaking away my offer of assistance, she clambered to her feet. "Get along with you," she said and waved my way to the streetcar like my personal valet. Yes, it was like that, personal.

I caught sight of her when we passed her by. Our eyes met in a flash and in less than a flash she was left behind. I thought it was recognition I'd seen in her eyes, of something we shared, something beyond the house where we'd both stayed for a short time, but maybe she was only telling me she'd seen me. She knew me. I'd always be the one watching from a streetcar passing by. Her eyes were an unusual dark, almost purple colour and full of earned intelligence. Later I thought they were the eyes of the betrayed boy in my dream, whose hand was lit on fire.

I was given a seat, and in fact was almost forced to take it, by a woman who was about thirty and whose mother stayed sitting beside me. Both women carried huge leather hand-bags that were so full they gaped. The mother kept hers on her lap; the daughter let hers swing by my face. Both women had missing front teeth. The middle two teeth on top. They had identical, endearing lisps, which they enjoyed showing off.

"Was that thscrag bothering you?" the daughter asked.

"Who?" I asked, not understanding her.

"That thscrag you were talking to on the thsidewalk," the mother explained. "We thaid, there thshe is harathing that poor woman." She patted my arm.

"Oh no. I just thought... she seemed sad."

"A uthser," the daughter said.

"Deprethion can lead to addicthion," the mother explained.

I wondered what could be done. "I mean, what works to help, to end the cycle."

"Dogths," the mother said.

"Dogs?"

"Petths," the daughter explained.

"Thomething to love," the mother said.

Apparently they found Dobermans extremely loyal. I fell to thinking about my mother, wondering if my behaviour towards her had been disloyal. We had never been as friendly as the two either side of me on the streetcar. They were so solicitous of me, I had the feeling while I sat between them that I had no volition and needed none. I could have travelled without a care across the city, across the world, between them.

At Yonge Street, where the man who fed the pigeons sat amongst them on his pigeon-shitty blanket, the mother and her daughter got off and a woman in a motorized scooter got on. It took a full minute for the driver and the teenaged boy who accompanied her to board her. Even using the lift, they had a time of it to hoist her on. The boy, with the wild black hair and the equally wild handsomeness of a teen porn star, appeared to be her caregiver. I thought maybe he was her grandson because she treated him like a slave, complaining all the time he settled her, and only some kind of helpless tie could explain his acquiescence. Her ball cap was rhinestoned and her sneakers were too.

"Where's my water?" she snapped.

I startled. She'd ended up parked facing me, just across the aisle.

"In your backpack," the grandson muttered.

"And?"

He opened the backpack and handed her the bottle of water. She waited until he'd unscrewed the cap and then she grunted and drank. The streetcar jerked to a stop; the boy jerked too and his arm hit her elbow. Water sloshed out of her bottle and onto her lap.

"Idiot!" she screamed. "Look at this." She pawed at her lap. "Come here." He backed off and hesitated; she gave him a look that brought him closer, and then, as he must have known she would, she sloshed the rest of her water into his face. He stayed standing beside her for a few moments, his head down, his long hair shielding his face.

"Born useless," she told the rest of us.

I thought I was observing it all surreptitiously, but she spotted me and hissed, "Who do you think you are?"

"Me?" I said. She did a good malevolent. I couldn't look away.

"Yeah. You!" she shouted.

"Hey, quiet down," the driver called out. He stopped hard at an amber light, as if to teach her a lesson. She knew it. "Asshole!" she hollered.

I thought of my mother. She'd railed at me, at everyone around her, during her last weeks. But she'd been out of her mind on morphine. She'd been in a panic, trying to control what was happening to her. I thought this must be what was going on with the woman in the scooter. I thought this was the way to think about her instead of deciding she was just a monster. Suddenly, while I was coming to that conclusion, she tilted in her scooter. Her arms flew up and her eyes rolled back. I could see only white in her eyes. I half rose from my seat. No one else moved to help her. Her grandson looked away. I didn't know what to do, so I was half standing, frozen like that, when as suddenly as she'd been stricken, she lowered her arms, set her hands on her fat knees, and grinned at me. "Gotcha!" she said quietly.

I sat down hard. Instinctively, I looked to her grandson, as if he could tell me how to react. By this time he was half sitting in his single left-hand seat and half hanging from the bar overhead. He was swinging back and forth. He didn't know how gorgeous he was in his glittery, messy youth, his long hair and his lithe limbs shining. Fuck you all, he said. He said it to himself, not out loud, but I heard him and agreed; yes that was what we should do. Anything else was useless.

But I could not stand it. I said, "This is the last straw."

She was still watching me to see if there was another morsel to be eaten. I said, "Why?"

She scoffed and rolled her eyes again, enough to show me she could scare me any time she liked, and then she turned away.

I wasn't having it. "Why? Why? Why? Why?" I'd started quietly, but once I got going and she still wouldn't look at me, I got louder. Pretty soon I was shouting. "Why? Why? Why?" I stood up and grabbed the pole beside my seat or I would have lost my balance. "*Why?*"

And then I heard the silence around me. Wow, I'd created it. But I wasn't done. "I want to know why."

"No kidding," she said, looking past me. Some guy behind me laughed.

I took a breath and steadied myself, looking down at her. "Why?"

She had the kind of eyes that could drill you. "I don't like you," she said. "I don't like the way you look at me. Staring at me. Take a look around, take a gander at this crowd." She jerked her head and I glanced around. The streetcar was about three-quarters full. Every single person I could see looked away.

"That's how you're supposed to look at people. You *don't* look. You mind your own fucking business, see? You don't *look* at people like you're storing them up for something you can tell your friends at *lunch*."

I sank down in my seat, had to slide my hand down the pole to do it or I would have fallen over.

"You're the one who needs help," she added.

"Yes." I was shaking so hard I could barely squeak.

The streetcar stopped. I said, "I think I do need help," but she wasn't listening.

The doors snapped open. I said, "I've never done anything like that before."

A young woman with a kid in a stroller boarded. A guy with a bandana tied around his head got on. The woman in the scooter didn't want to let the woman with the stroller past; it didn't mean she had to move the scooter or pull her rhinestoned feet in an inch or two; she only had to pull her elbow closer to her side and the stroller could have got through. It looked like a draw, but the little one started crying, and she must have decided having them beside her would be worse than the pleasure of unkindness. After them, the guy in the bandana bopped past, his music in his ears, on his face. And then I knew: *I never learn*. Nike woman tried to tell me, but I never learn. You don't *look* at people.

I wanted to tell the woman in the scooter I understood what she was saying, but just then someone I recognized— the tiny woman with the bright white braids and the colourful apparel, the one who had told me she sometimes wanted to hit people—climbed up the steps and flipped her pass. Serenely ignoring everyone else, she sailed up to me. "Hey," she said, "you're the lady from Saskatchewan."

"Christ," the woman in the scooter said. "That explains it."

"You're the woman who sometimes feels like hitting someone," I said.

That got a nod somewhere between amusement and approval.

"Would you like my seat?" I asked. "I need to get off soon."

She motioned me to stay where I was and swayed beside me. She was old, maybe as old as eighty, but wiry, her body compact and tough. Her face relaxed easily into its good humour lines. "I do often feel like hitting someone," she said, with her bright eyes on the woman in the scooter. "But due to my former profession, I have great self-discipline." She had been a schoolteacher, she said, proud of it. A dozen boys climbed on, ploughed their way to the back, and started enjoying being boisterous. She turned to them and put her finger to her lips and for some reason they quieted down. "Good boys," she said.

I loved that little woman.

I got off at the next stop. My legs felt weak, and I wasn't sure where I was, but I'd stayed on the streetcar longer than I'd intended and knew I must be farther west than my destination. I only had to walk back along the sidewalk until I found the unnamed place (unnamed, that is, in my memory) that I now realized I was looking for.

———————

It wasn't luck that I got the same table and was able to sit exactly where I had before; the café was empty but for the waiter. The most interesting thing in the place was the grit on the floor, brought in on the soles of the few who had entered that day, ground fine by their trainers' performance polymer. A mere six weeks had elapsed since I'd sat there before. I ordered a chai latte, of course, and went over what was said the last time I sat there, what it meant, how it felt, what I might have missed, and what it signified that Ryan and Aubrey had been such pals.

I'd already guessed much of the scam. It was painful to go over it and fill in the blanks, to see again how Ryan's face, with that assumed boredom printed on it, grew eager. He had set me up from the start. He knew about me and easily guessed my interest in writing Marianne Rasmussen's biography. That was why he'd interviewed me for his article on regionalism, to find out if it was true, and to ascertain how far I'd delved into the project. It could only have been for one reason: he was interested in writing her biography too. He'd admitted that later. But I didn't understand why he'd led me to the Ash brothers. All I knew was that it wasn't for a good reason, not good for me.

The waiter slipped into the kitchen. Probably didn't like the broody look of me. I glared at the minimalist tables and uncomfortable wire chairs. I imagined the grit swept up and pouring through an hourglass, inexorably, while the waiter sat on his stool in the kitchen and looked at himself in the glass door of the freezer where they kept the fresh-baked pastries. I let my tea get cold.

---

I didn't have the strength to get on a streetcar again, so when I left the café I started walking back to Ontario Street. From the get-go I dragged my feet. Somewhere since the corner store, way the other end of downtown, Marianne had left me. She had seldom visited me in the last weeks, but I'd never felt deserted until now. I couldn't pinpoint where it had happened that she'd completely left, but I was pretty sure she wasn't coming back.

I moved through the crowd on the sidewalk, heading east. The day wasn't near sunset yet; nothing metaphorical was going on, and I felt it never would. I felt I wouldn't ever again find my own wee happiness in making quick connections, likening one thing to another with a ping of personal satisfaction. I was through with pretending to be the poet I couldn't be, through with pretending I had a mentor angel looking over me. Aubrey was right: I had nothing inside me for a key to unlock. I had never had the talent or the vitality or the vision to take me to competency let alone brilliance.

There was another reason for my distress, and my mind strayed to it; it was an ache that made itself known, hovering in the background of all other thoughts, and then once in a while piercing me with a pain so sharp even with my dulled senses I gasped. It was that Harry had been a part of the scheme. He had known about it and had not informed me. And that morning, knowing what was on my mind, knowing how desperately I wanted those documents of Aubrey's, he'd said nothing.

Again and again, I went back to the moment the night before when he sat beside me on Aubrey's bed and tried to hold my hand. I knew then that he'd betrayed me. Everyone betrays you in the end; what's new about that? But it meant it was the end. I would return to the house, I would pack my things into my bag, we would talk, yes we would talk, and then I would go. I already understood I wouldn't get any of the letters or the photos or anything else Aubrey had saved that had come from Marianne Rasmussen. You know when you're finished.

The day was waning and people had errands to do. They brushed past me, sometimes against me, without ever making eye contact. I didn't look at them either. I walked on, eastward, with the smell of downtown in my nostrils, the smell of generations of defeat that had permeated the pavement. Cars honked, brakes squealed, bikers yelled their warnings, people swore and laughed. I picked up my pace. I walked on like an urbanite, deliberately, undeviating in my path, past big windows and small windows, glossy glass and smeared glass, past tall buildings and miserable huts made into businesses that were sure to fail, past intersections and alleys and parking lot exits, past every type of shoe imaginable and all kinds of grit, past subway stations and dozens of streetcar stops. I walked for so long I forgot I wasn't invisible. I walked through space like I was nothing. If there was anyone on that long trudge back to Ontario Street who might have treated me like a human being, or might have been treated like one by me, I didn't see them.

---

"Have you had dinner?" he asked when I got back. His voice was solemn; he wasn't going to pretend nothing had happened.

I hadn't eaten all day but said I was all right and poured myself a glass of wine. I held up the bottle and he nodded and I poured one for him too. A loaf of bread was on the table along with a triangle of cheese, and silently we ate. Neither of us mentioned going out to sit in the garden.

"My meeting today was with Aubrey's lawyer," he said finally.

"That was quick."

He ignored the disparagement in my comment. "It was all set in advance. Aubrey knew he didn't have long; he knew it would be soon. We both believed you extended his life, actually, by a few weeks."

I ignored that comment.

"I hadn't known what was in his will," he said. "But I could have guessed, and by now I expect you can too."

"Hardly worth speaking of," I murmured.

"I'm sorry. I know how much you hoped—"

"Just say it."

"The letters and photos, everything goes to Ryan Benson. He's writing the biography."

"Of Aubrey Ash?" I was determined to make him say it.

Harry cleared his throat. It was a habit of his, as it is of many people, many men, when they have to admit a thing they would rather not admit.

I waited.

"Of Marianne Rasmussen," he said. His voice had gone quiet, and he cleared his throat again.

"And you knew," I said. "You knew all along."

"I knew and I didn't tell you. I won't ask you to forgive me. It wasn't out of loyalty to Aubrey. The truth is, I thought you'd go. If you'd known, you wouldn't have stuck it out, would you? You'd have left, and I wanted you to stay."

He poured us both another glass of wine. I vowed not to touch mine.

"Can we talk about this?" he asked.

I gazed into my glass.

"I know how you must feel," he said.

"You have no idea how I feel," I said.

"I think we could get to the bottom of this."

"Oh I'm past the bottom."

"But, listen," he said. "I've thought about this moment often in the past weeks. I knew it had to come to this. And when you showed me your story, I felt I could explain. If you'll listen. I want to ask you, do you think your interest in this particular phase of Marianne Rasmussen's life had to do with her dropping Aubrey? Leaving him for someone else? Or going back to her husband, whatever it was? Walking out on Aubrey? Dumping him?"

At first I wasn't going to answer; I didn't want to sit there chatting over wine. I wanted to have a big scene, throw the glassful in his face, knock him over the head with the bottle, or failing physical violence, stand over him screaming. And there he was looking at me as if with an honest face.

"You mean was I interested because Marianne spurned him. Humiliated him. Because she wrecked the fragile thing they'd built together. You mean I, specifically, particularly—being me—wanted to explore that topic."

I sat back and thought for a minute, calming myself, and it seemed to me I was being truthful, and that I was capable of saying what I thought without it being dyed black with all the strangling bad emotion I was keeping in check. "But any biographer would go after it, you know. Anyone would seek out the drama in a life. You look for the seeds of discontent and then for the fruit of despair, so to speak. How it affects the writing, that's what you're after, in a literary biography."

"So nothing personal about it," Harry said.

"I get your point, I do, but Harry, it's life, isn't it? Loving and losing. What else is there of any importance? And writing. For a writer. But what do we write about? Loving and losing, one way or another, that's it."

"I love you," he said.

I laughed.

I didn't drink my second glass of wine. I saw his face and I stood up and left the room. I packed my bag and called a cab and went to the airport to wait for a standby flight home.

Elizabeth Bishop has a great poem about the art of losing. At Toronto Pearson, I found it through Google and read it over a hundred times. Yes, this felt like a disaster.

# { 14 }

AFTER I'D BEEN HOME for a few days, I surfaced from my first round of depression and decided taking umbrage might save me. I texted Ryan Benson. I pictured him togged in his limp scarf, strolling along the Seine, hearing his phone chime. I didn't expect he would answer; I had no idea what time it would be in Paris.

You would have thought we were friends by his response. Maybe he was lonely, feeling dark in the city of light; maybe he had a smidgeon of a conscience and it relieved him to bare all; or maybe he just liked the chance to gloat. Before he could enjoy himself too much, I said it was probably wrong to make the affair with Aubrey the centre of Marianne's biography. The idea that a woman poet might owe her inspiration to a male lover or muse was passé. The real question, I said, wasn't how a relationship with a man had changed her, but how she had changed her poetry to transcend the grip of the patriarchy. Ryan was pleased to agree. He was pleased to let me know, now that the truth could be told, that he was in Paris researching a two-week vacation Marianne had taken with her husband the year before she died. Not a muse, Ryan said—no one would accuse old Irv of that—but possibly an enabler. Some rather nice poems had come from the trip, he said. And it was his good fortune to be granted four months to research her two weeks. A lovely irony, he called it.

I was too proud to ask about the mechanism of the scheme he and Aubrey had enacted, but I didn't have to ask; Ryan emailed me the details less than an hour later. In his elation over being granted all the Rasmussen documents, he didn't seem to have any concern over revealing how he'd finagled them. Seen from the point of view of hindsight, it was a simple plan, and one I didn't need to take personally, he implied, since it had been set into action before he ever knew of my existence. (Ryan was never very careful about anyone's self-concept, and victorious as he'd proven himself to be, he wasn't going to start worrying now about slighting me.)

Before he met with me, before he'd contacted me about the interview on regionalism, Ryan had made an agreement with Aubrey that he would live in the Ontario Street house and help the brothers out, both by paying rent and by doing kitchen duty. Aubrey had been worried that Harry was getting tired of carrying the load himself. "It wouldn't have been for long," Ryan wrote, "and in exchange he promised me all the Rasmussen papers. I was willing, but then I got the Paris gig. I couldn't give that up. We discussed the problem and I said I'd find a substitute to look after them, someone who would pay the rent he asked and cook and all that. He didn't really have a choice—I mean I was going to Paris, I wasn't going to give that up—and anyway once he heard about you (he thought it audacious of you to write about Marianne) the idea intrigued him—the switcheroo, you know, that you thought you were duping him while he was duping you. A little end-of-life game, he called it, and it worked beautifully, you know, thanks to you. Will you write her biography anyway?" he asked. The jerk.

"No," I replied. "I'm going to write his." This was a piece of nonsense, but Ryan took it seriously and responded: "I have no need of Aubrey's old files that have nothing to do with Marianne and will be only too happy to hand them over to you." The triple jerk.

I had a question: "Was Harry in on the whole thing?"

The answer was: "He thought you and I were partners, that I was going to share the papers with you. I'm sorry to have to declare he was wrong about that; I may have misled him, and I'm pretty sure Aubrey did."

I envisioned strangling Ryan at that point. I could feel the damp silk in my fingers, my fingers as taut as Aubrey's old claws. One good wrench and I could hear him gagging. Still, Harry was not exonerated; he had been in on a good part of the enterprise. I remembered his big smile the day we met, and how the lights went on in his eyes as if he'd recognized me the moment he saw me. What had he meant by that? I'd thought he'd seen into me, and I suppose he had, but in a different way than I divined at the time. He wasn't seeing the real me, he was seeing Ryan Benson's partner, come to cook and clean. No wonder the smile was so welcoming.

Yes, he was happy to see me at his door, happy to let me prattle on about the garden, and he'd enjoyed getting me flustered about the details regarding the renting of a room. Or maybe he really was confused by some of the things I said that didn't jibe with what he'd heard from Ryan and Aubrey. He hadn't liked Ryan, that was clear, and it was a point in his favour.

I remembered his ten-minute absence from the house, the first time I'd known him to go out, that had seemed mysterious to me. Probably it had been nothing but an errand for Aubrey, maybe to mail a letter to Ryan Benson; that would have been enough to upset Harry and alert me. But he did it; he went along with Ryan and Aubrey. He knew they were using me. And there I was castigating myself for being unscrupulous. I was willing to see myself as unethical, and to pay for it, but to have the tables turned, to be the dupe—such a fool—that really stung.

I could not keep going over and over all the instances in which I'd been an idiot, thinking I was a player when I was being played. I had to sweep up this whole mess, apportion blame, and end the agony. Yes, I'd treated Harry badly; I'd set out to infatuate him, and look at the result. But he'd hardly treated me fairly. Well then, we were even. We'd evenly deceived each other. From now on, I decided, I was going to ignore that last look on his face. It wasn't up to me to interpret that expression or think there was anything I could ever do to atone. That face was going to fade from my memory. Soon it would be gone.

I also decided that what Ryan had suggested wasn't completely out of line. If he handed over Aubrey's papers I would have all I needed to write Aubrey's biography. I had my notes and the recorded conversations downloaded on my laptop. It was a fit; it suited me. I figured I was more like Aubrey than I would care to admit. He was always spouting Bellow; I wished I could be Rasmussen. Frustrated writers, both of us. And so I reread his fiction. I had nothing else to do: my own writing was on hold, my brain was doing the whirring thing, my mixed-up emotions engulfed me. Only another person's words could lift me, if only temporarily, out of the pit. And Aubrey's stories were good; they were very good. I thought he deserved another look, a reassessment. He would have appreciated the irony. How his old shoulders would have risen and fallen. I could hear his wheezy old laugh. But after all, I had all kinds of knowledge of him and his life. It wouldn't be as sexy as the Rasmussen biography; it wouldn't make my fortune. But I needed a book, and in my determination to recover, I told myself it was one I could write.

---

If willpower could design a life I would have been fine. But in my own home, the house on Ontario Street haunted me. In my own kitchen I reached for utensils in the places they would have been found in those cupboards. Walking up the stairs to my second floor, I turned, surprised to find no flight to a third. Worse, much worse, my mind was tormented by knowledge I couldn't deny. I couldn't get over knowing that Ryan and Aubrey had used me because they could, that my desire to get the papers had overcome my good sense as well as my scruples.

They all saw through me. Aubrey saw through me. Even if he hadn't known everything in advance, he would have seen through me. The key to brilliant composition. Had I really believed it could be found in those papers, or anywhere else? But it was written all over my face how much I wanted it. Ryan too, he saw it. How amused they must have been when I gloated, thinking I'd had some small triumph, when all the time, every day, I'd been exposed for who I was and what I pitiably wasn't.

---

I went on for some days jumping my mind through hoops, generally making myself crazy. I refused my friends' invitations; I didn't want my situation subjected to anyone else's analysis, not even of a caring kind. Now and then X texted me. He'd found out I'd returned and wanted to express his relief and continued concern, his regret for the past. I gathered that Suzanne was no longer in the picture.

So he was lonely.

---

I spent my time reading when I could, drifting when I couldn't. No amount of mild weather could seduce me out of the house, and then one day the sky sank low, like a bruise I could see from every window. Inside my house the air rubbed me, and it rubbed me wrong. All the rooms went dark in the middle of the afternoon, and I didn't turn the lights on. As day progressed to evening and still the sky glowered, I found candles and matches and set them on my dining room table. I sat there waiting, listening for thunder.

I poured myself a double scotch and thought about my mother and her anger at me when I wouldn't talk to her. At the time I didn't see my denial of her as cruel. Her need was another assault on my integrity—that was how I saw it then, or I should say that was how I felt it then. I saw nothing clearly. My poor mother. She thought the end of my marriage might mean the end of me. She was hurt as well as angry when I refused to talk to her, and when things got back to normal and I tried to talk to her again, she stayed hurt and angry. Her face looked wary the last time I saw her. Her voice sounded wary. I didn't try very hard to overcome that. I thought time would soften her.

And now, when it was too late, while I listened for thunder, I listened too for her voice, or even just her breath, for the intake of her breath, the small pop of lips on cigarette, inhalation, pause, sigh. It had been a long time since I'd wished for her sympathy, but I wished I could have her with me while I waited for the storm to break. I would have poured her a rye and water in a crystal glass. No ice—watch her impatiently wave ice away. In my own glass, scotch on the rocks. Listen to it tinkle, my own little noise into the night. I would have told her I didn't do it to be mean. Something in me had closed. I couldn't let anyone in. A form of self-protection. Never let them know how much you care.

My mother didn't come to sit at my candlelit table; the storm didn't break. I had another glass of scotch and then I went to my desk and opened my laptop. I had the idea I'd send X my biographer story, see what he'd say about it, if he'd even answer me. "The Art of Biography," could have been titled "The Art of Losing." I stared at the screen until it went black and I had another thought. It was that Harry had been wrong about my story. He'd seen me as A in a story about A and B, the marriage of A and B, the failure of their love. But I wasn't A. I wasn't the person who was angry at having my life invaded. Or maybe I was A when I wrote the story, but it was an old story, and by the time I came to the house on Ontario Street, I was the biographer, the one who wanted to open others' lives and peer in. But not just to witness and not just to document. I wanted to take part. I was the poor puny biographer huddled on the front step, a pitiable creature without a love and a life of my own.

And yet—

There was comfort in this way of thinking. I wasn't A. It was an old story. It didn't need any commentary from X. Such a gentle feeling of relief came to me when I sat back, closed the laptop, heard the muted clap of top to bottom, the sound of shutting down.

164

All these thoughts came to me as I sat at my dining room table and no storm came to clear the air and the evening turned into night and the candles guttered out, as anyone might have predicted they would do, to a single one.

———————

After some time, the dullness I lived with lifted a little and I started finding ways towards revival. Partly these ways had to do with cups of tea and glasses of wine, quilts on rainy days and sunbathing nude behind my hedges on sunny days, the last sunny days of that summer. I began to let all these forms of warmth actually warm me. I went to my book-shelves for my poets, Emily Dickinson first and then others at random. Better than my consolations were the trips my mind started taking again, the thoughts and memories that words or sights or smells surprised in me. Grating a lemon for risotto one evening, I remembered hearing Harry whistle. He was outside in the garden. X used to whistle too, once in a while, when he was alone. It made me think there's a special kind of bravery demanded of men in our society, and how I might use the flip side of that bravery, the posturing it could lead to, in a story. I started making all kinds of observations that amused me, and letting the tiniest events turn into nar-ratives, even sometimes into tentative poems. I didn't start work on Aubrey's biography; I didn't feel strong enough to combat the letdown that still threatened when I remembered what I'd lost, but I thought I soon would.

I missed Harry more than I could have imagined. I missed his laugh, and the desire and the ability to make him laugh. I missed watching him for however he would respond to any and every little thing that happened. I missed his voice and his touch. But at the same time I thought I'd escaped. Hadn't I? If I was ever going to write anything worthwhile, now was the time. I was free of my obligation to Marianne, free of my overweening ambition to write the poems she'd already written. And I was free of men. No relationship had any claim on me.

———————

A friend called and insisted I meet her for lunch; she said she needed advice. Even the downhearted can seldom refuse the temptation to advise, and besides I was getting tired of my own company. The counselling part of the meeting didn't take long. It was an old problem she was dealing with, and soon I began telling her about my last day at the Ash brothers' house.

"The Ash brothers," she murmured, opening her menu.

"I've finished my research on Marianne Rasmussen, by the way. I've given up on the idea. Of writing the biography."

"I'm glad. You were obsessed with that woman, you know."

That rankled, but I decided to brush it off. It's the way of old friends to make up stories about one another and then stick to them. I went on telling her about my last day in Toronto and the people I'd met when I was out wandering like some kind of lost cloud. "I was waiting to catch a streetcar and a woman with a wounded arm staggered up to me and fell at my feet. Flat out on the sidewalk, at my feet. And said she knew me. She did too; she was one of the people who were involved in a break-in, a knife fight in the house next door."

My friend looked up from her menu and said she would have the chicken and brie sandwich, as she always did. And a large glass of Sauvignon Blanc. I agreed I would have the same. I went on telling her about my streetcar companions, the Transit Women I was calling them, the mother and daughter with the teeth knocked out, and the woman in the scooter. Our wine arrived and we lifted our glasses, smiled at one another, and sipped. And the little old woman who sometimes felt like hitting someone, naturally I spoke of her too. I said I thought of her as a philosopher.

"Do you ever think you're living more than one life?" I asked my friend. "That's not quite what I mean. That our lives are connected in ways we normally don't think about? That we are actually part of one another? I just remembered what the woman in the scooter said to me. 'Who do you think you are?' And what famous Canadian writer does that bring to mind? The other woman I told you about, the one on the sidewalk, her arm was wounded, and now I'm wondering if it was her writing arm. 'I know you,' she said to me. It's the same thing Aubrey said when we first met."

I was only half being silly, only half trying to amuse my friend, and she gave me a look that said she knew exactly what I was doing, if I didn't. She said, "Maybe all these incidents are just things that happened to you on the way from one place to another."

"Do you mean it might not all be about me? I thought they might have been trying to tell me something."

"You're just trying to understand what happened to you. I mean, it wasn't nothing."

"I wanted to be a match for those men."

My friend looked at me with her head to the side, the good-friend-waiting pose.

"I imagined my mother coming to visit me. Sat her right down with me, poured her a drink. Imagined her telling me I was a match for the men." My friend didn't jump in at this point to tell a story of her own, as I would probably have

167

done; she waited, giving me a chance to think aloud. "Was I a match for the men? Did I need to be? Is that what my mother taught me? Is that why I keep thinking of the Transit Women? Because that was their struggle? To be a match for men? I wasn't, obviously. I was no match for Ryan and Aubrey."

"They say writing is the best revenge."

"They also say if you can't win, change the rules of the game."

My friend folded her napkin. I'd barely realized I'd eaten my sandwich. I said, "I'm starting to wonder if I have a single thought of my own. I'm so influenced by everyone. From my mother on down."

Across the room, an older man was sitting alone, sipping soup. He'd tucked his napkin into his shirt collar; it appeared to have been a good idea. "I wish I didn't get so tangled in people," I said to my friend. "I mean, they're everywhere. You can't get away from them."

We each took a last sip of our wine. I wondered what Harry was doing now, this very instant. I pictured him sitting alone at the table by the window that looked out on the garden. Rubbing at his forehead. Thinking his own thoughts.

"Men can think their own thoughts," I said.

"All of society thinks men's thoughts," my friend said.

I got out my credit card and set it beside hers. The man across the room removed his napkin from his collar, flapped it with a flourish, and winked at me. My friend raised her eyebrows when I turned back to her.

"Why does it always feel like a capitulation?" I asked.

"Because it is. But it is for men too—I mean the real thing."

"You know what?" I asked my friend.

"No, I don't," she said.

"I've been behaving like the perfect little housewife, trying to tidy everything up."

"And?"

"I have one more thing to do."

I could still see Harry. He was sitting where he always sat, whether the chair across from him was occupied or empty.

# { 15 }

I HAD TO SEND A LETTER to Harry since he didn't have email and I didn't dare phone him. What would I have said? "I'm coming to Toronto next week," I wrote, "and on the 7th of October, about seven o'clock in the evening, I plan to visit the Dickies of the Necropolis to see how they are faring."

It seemed right to arrive at dusk, at twilight time, to walk into the cemetery and see autumn leaves falling, a few every minute. I didn't know if Harry would come to meet me; I'd sent the letter the week before, and if he had responded, his answer wouldn't have reached my mailbox by the time I left for Toronto. I had planned it that way, not wanting to make it a plan, just letting myself wonder.

I stood at the entrance to the grounds, under the Gothic archway, for a minute, thinking about Aubrey Ash. I didn't know whether or not he was buried there. I thought about lying to him, telling him on his birthday that I would write his biography. I was never going to write that book. His stories were more inspiring than his life was. They were full of his idiosyncratic charm, his zest, his greediness for life. They'd made me think how personal all writing is, how hard it is to get it right, and how little time a person has.

170

The leaves drifted down; a few of them were gold; the rest were still green but they were getting ready to let go. I remembered Louise Glück's poem about the evening star, the single light in a black night, a light with the power to console. Poetry had shone that light in my life; it had allowed me to recoup myself a hundred times over, to step outside of the limits of self and see again how beautiful the earth is, how oddly intoxicating it is to watch the sky darken, the leaves float down. At times like this, meaning doesn't matter. Or do I mean that matter has its own meaning? Simply, there are times when being is enough.

But I had a mission, and now that I'd arrived, a mundane problem arose; I realized I didn't have a perfect idea of where the Dickie grave was located. I knew it was by a path because I remembered standing close beside Harry, our arms touching, and I remembered looking down at our feet planted on cement. I remembered knowing we were smiling the same smiles. We had discovered a memory we shared.

The evening was cool with a breeze that wanted to do some mischief, but I was warmly dressed and welcomed the rustle above me and the leaves sifting across my vision. I had come early enough that I didn't need to worry I'd be late. The Necropolis, like every place on earth, has its boundaries, and I had time to find the Dickie tombstone within them. Soon, though, I started feeling as rootless as the leaves, as fragile and as ready to fall to the ground, and I knew why. I had not mastered the art of losing. I was searching, peering along the paths, not knowing which way to turn. I was hurrying, whichever way I turned, down one path and then another, sending my hope ahead of me. And so strong was my hope and so determined, even if not exactly rational, that I didn't realize I wasn't looking at the gravestones, I wasn't looking for the stones or the names on them, I was looking over them, past them. I had my sights set higher, and fortunately for me I was proven to be right in doing that. Just when it seemed that the cemetery had become a maze and I might be late for the meeting I'd set up, I found what I was looking for. Halfway down a long walkway, a tall tree was standing by the Dickies, marking their spot.

----

He watched me run to him. He did not, as in some romantic film, hold out his arms or even extend a hand, but I thought he looked fondly on me.

"Harry!"

He smiled down at the path.

"I'm so glad!" I stopped abruptly before I got close enough to embrace him. I couldn't finish my sentence, the words I'd intended to say. There was nothing forbidding in his mien; it wasn't anything he was doing that stopped me. But he was different from how I'd remembered him. He looked frailer than I remembered. He looked older. A gust buffeted him and he flinched. It did feel cold.

"I worried you wouldn't come," I said.

"Here I am."

I was afraid to ask him how he was, how things were. I found myself searching his face for signs that he'd been through a fire. I had, in a dream, stood on the sidewalk on Ontario Street watching the radiant light of flames brighten every window of the Ash house and the twin next door. I'd seen the entire house collapse. It had seemed so real I thought its correlative must have happened; something must have wounded him. But no, he was no Rochester. No scars, no scorched eyebrows, no blinded eye. In his face there was a mirroring or a recognition of what I was feeling. I wasn't as he'd remembered me either.

"It's cold, isn't it?" I said. "The sun's gone down. Let's go somewhere? There's a little bar isn't there, a few blocks away?"

"You're looking well," he said.

I listened for the caress and tried to convince myself it was there in his voice, that we were simply, understandably, awkward together. We needed a little time to get used to each other, that was all. It will be all right once we get talking, I thought.

"We have so much to talk about," I said. I felt I should take hold of his arm and start us walking out of the cemetery, but I didn't feel brave enough. I talked instead while he stood shivering. "I've thought things through. Everything was so convoluted. It was quite a puzzle. For me, I mean. In the end I just thought I should—give up. Think about what matters."

There it was, that big, generous smile. It extended to his mild blue eyes.

"Remember the woman who attacked me here?" I asked. "For taking pictures of her when she was planting a grave?"

He nodded.

"Now there was a woman who knew what mattered." That wasn't a tenth of what I meant to say, but we were shivering; there wasn't time for explanations.

"I have something for you," he said. He unzipped his jacket and took out a manila envelope. A five-by-seven size. The wind shook it as he held it out.

"Let's wait until we get inside," I said.

He slipped it back into his jacket. He took my arm and hooked it through his. So he led me with old-fashioned courtesy, and we left the Dickies and the Necropolis. I asked him a few questions of a general nature as we walked out. He answered them by saying his health was fine, the house was still standing, the neighbourhood had not much changed, or if it had he hadn't noticed. When we reached the tavern he stopped and brought the envelope out from his jacket again. "I saved one thing for you," he said.

"Come," I said, moving to the door. I set my hand on the doorknob.

He handed me the envelope; I had no choice but to take it, but still hoping, I kept hold of the doorknob.

"I wish you all the best," he said gently. Ah, there was the caress. His kind blue eyes said he meant it to be there. He was solicitous too when he walked away; when he reached the corner he looked back and smiled at me and waved a little salute.

# { 16 }

I FIND MYSELF TURNING more often now to the poems of Marianne Rasmussen's later years. They are quieter than her earlier work but still powerful, and from my new perspective they seem wiser. Probably that only means they're the kind of poems I need now. Yet it seems to me that Rasmussen's late work has a lustre that the earlier, headier poems don't have, a gentle emanation that seeps from between the words with appealing candour, like a smile of satisfaction you might catch on your own face while you watch some unknown member of the human race behaving accidentally lovably. I think of Irv, to whom the last book is dedicated, and his cousin, who said to me: "You are wondering about my hat. I wore it in case his spirit is still hovering, to give him courage." Yes, I find the later poems heartening.

How strange it is that our lives are not usefully taken apart, not instructive in their compartments, but everything in one life is twisted inextricably with everything else, and it's impossible to decipher it all. I am thinking how language uses us. Earlier, I wrote that Rasmussen's passionate poetry was heady, and now I'm calling the quieter poems heartening.

I'm looking forward to reading Ryan Benson's book on Marianne Rasmussen, although I think it won't be the book

I hoped to write. Neither—truth to tell—will my new publication be the book I hoped to write, but I feel with the next one I really am on the cusp of accomplishment, I really could write something that satisfies me. Even in a small way, even momentarily. That's the hope. Not to thrill the world or earn its accolades, but to end the yearning, even if only for one perfect line, one perfect phrase, two words that go pop when they come into contact.

In the envelope Harry gave me was, of course, the photograph of Marianne that Aubrey had taunted me with. I knew as soon as I drew it out of the envelope that day in the tavern and set it beside my glass of red wine; a glance was enough to tell me it was the one he'd had in mind. I also knew, before I saw it, that the photograph wouldn't be the kind of picture I'd thought I wanted for my book; Harry would not have given me that one. But it is revealing. Aubrey wasn't mistaken in that. It's a candid photo, head and shoulders, in colour. Of course it's in colour. It's of her laughing—laughing openly, unguardedly, from sheer love of life. I held her up that day in the tavern and gazed at her while she laughed, her face open, her eyes alive with feeling, as if she were looking into the eyes of someone she loved. Or as if she had escaped the plot—if they are not the same thing.

---

Often when I think of Marianne Rasmussen, I feel the same submerging grief I experienced in Toronto. It's not the loss of the papers and the ability to write the biography that I regret the most; it's the disquieting sense of a deeper loss, deeper even than the loss of someone to love. It's a kind of thin, hidden passion running underground like an underground stream, like music. I think of Tchaikovsky's "Andante Cantabile," a song that puts its shy hand out, or more tentatively a finger, and when I think of it, the tenderness at the base of real passion rises in me like that old loved piece of quiet music that, like all music, has to end. I tell myself there are no punch lines, there is no big joke, the puzzle itself is the solution, I am living my own life. But I am not sure it is true.

# { 17 }

I HAD JUST TOLD MY FRIEND I'd written the perfect ending to my Toronto story, a real Jamesian ending, when the waitress came to the table. She had an early sixties vibe, a shift dress, killer black eyeliner, and backcombing. She smelled like toast. I remembered something I'd forgotten.

My friend saw my excitement on my face. "What?" she asked. In the weeks that had passed since we'd last met, she'd gone back to her shaggier eyebrows, but she still looked ready to be amused.

"A revelation," I said. "I've just had a revelation."

"Something to drink?" the waitress asked, setting the menus down.

I leaned across the table. "It just came home to me now. The ending's perfect, but the book is wrong."

The waitress sighed. We each ordered a glass of Sauvignon Blanc.

I said, "The narrator kept seeing an old man with a cane. I think he was Henry James. I mean an embodiment of Henry James come to haunt the narrative, to keep the story in line. Or why else did she keep seeing him? He didn't like all the stray people who had no place in his novel and really, when

I think about it, didn't have much excuse for being in mine. I mean, I was supposed to focus on Aubrey and Harry."

"The Ash brothers," my friend murmured.

"At first my story fit into the Aspern plot. Writing it was a bit like living off to the side of reality, like painting over someone else's painting so bits show through, or covering it all and then feeling lost, the new painting staring at you like someone else's dog."

My friend has always had a dog for a companion. She nodded, happy to relate.

"At first it was fun to be part of the plot. I didn't realize how hard I was working to sustain the illusion, to keep on keeping my head above water." I was thinking of Goya's dog treading water, a painting my friend doesn't like. I'd learned she didn't like it when I gave her a bookmark with the image on it, saying wasn't it like writing. "But that's what I was doing. Treading water while the men floated by. I wanted to write a story where the woman wins, where she gets to write her book and gets the man too, and I still don't understand why it wasn't possible."

The waitress brought our wine. She had red fingernails so glossy they looked as wet as the wine.

My friend passed her menu to the waitress. "I'll have the chicken and brie," she said.

I held my hand up; I hadn't quite decided. "I made the men too old to start with. I can see that now," I said.

The waitress said she'd come back. I liked the way she said it, like she was a real person with a personality of her own.

I said, "I felt sorry for Aubrey in the end. He was supposed to be the artist, and she was supposed to be the muse, that's the way it was in his world, but she turned the tables on him."

179

"That was her revenge."

"I don't think she needed revenge. I wish I could have done better, I mean with the plot. I did stray badly. I put in a lot of stuff that didn't belong, stuff that actually happened. I got distracted."

"It's not a bad thing to be distracted by life."

I had to think about that. We sipped at our wine, companionably silent for a few minutes the way old friends can be.

The waitress came back to our table. I picked up my menu.

"Hey, I just thought of something. The old man with the cane wasn't Henry James. Couldn't have been. He wouldn't box a writer into a corner or even into one house. I just thought of something he said, his advice to writers. He said, 'All life belongs to you.' All life."

The waitress folded her arms and sighed a big, dramatic, the-world-could-be-ending sigh. She had a cute pouchy stomach, such as only the young can get away with, and a hipbone poked into her shift like a misplaced comma.

# { Afterword }

"But why not? Who's afraid?"

Henry James
from his notes on *The Ivory Tower*
Unfinished novel, posthumously published in 1917

CONNIE GAULT has written for stage and radio and film. Her first novel, *Euphoria*, won a Saskatchewan Book Award for Fiction and was short-listed for the High Plains Fiction Award and the Commonwealth Prize for Best Book of Canada and the Caribbean. *A Beauty* won the 2016 Saskatchewan Book of the Year as well as the award for fiction, and was long-listed for the Scotiabank Giller Prize. A former prose editor of *Grain* magazine, Connie has also edited books of fiction and has taught many creative writing classes and mentored emerging writers. After spending most of her life in Saskatchewan, she now lives in London, Ontario.